Forever a Strang

HELLA S. HAASSE

Forever a Stranger and Other Stories

Translated from the Dutch and Introduced by
MARGARET M. ALIBASAH

KUALA LUMPUR
OXFORD UNIVERSITY PRESS
OXFORD   SINGAPORE   NEW YORK
1996

Oxford University Press

Oxford New York
Athens Auckland Bangkok Bombay
Calcutta Cape Town Dar es Salaam Delhi
Florence Hong Kong Istanbul Karachi
Madras Madrid Melbourne Mexico City
Nairobi Paris Shah Alam Singapore
Taipei Tokyo Toronto

and associated companies in
Berlin Ibadan

Oxford is a trade mark of Oxford University Press

Published in the United States
by Oxford University Press, New York

'Forever a Stranger' first published as 'Oeroeg' by Em. Querido's
Uitgeverij B. V., Amsterdam © Hella S. Haasse 1948
'Lidah Boeaja (Crocodile's Tongue)' and 'An Affair (Egbert's Story)'
first published as 'De Lidah Boeaja' and 'Een perkara
(Het Verhaal van Egbert)' in Een handvol achtergrond by
Em. Querido's Uitgeverij B. V., Amsterdam
© Hella S. Haasse 1993
English translation © Margaret M. Alibasah 1996

British Library Cataloguing in Publication Data
Data available

Library of Congress Cataloging-in-Publication Data
Haasse, Hella S., 1918–
[Short stories. English. Selections]
Forever a stranger and other stories/Hella S. Haasse:
translated from the Dutch by Margaret M. Alibasah.
p. cm.
Contents: Forever a stranger—Lidah Boeaja (Crocodile's tongue)
— An affair (Egbert's story).
ISBN 983 56 0003 1
1. Haasse, Hella S., 1918– —Translations into English.
2. Indonesia—Fiction.
I. Alibasah, Margaret M. II. Title.
PT5838. H45A23 1996
839.3'1364—dc20
96-7736
CIP

Typeset by Indah Photosetting Centre Sdn. Bhd., Malaysia
Printed by KHL Printing Co. (S) Pte. Ltd., Singapore
Published by the South-East Asian Publishing Unit,
a division of Penerbit Fajar Bakti Sdn. Bhd.,
under licence from Oxford University Press,
4 Jalan U1/15, Seksyen U1, 40000 Shah Alam,
Selangor Darul Ehsan, Malaysia

Contents

Introduction

HELLA S. HAASSE is one of Holland's most prolific contemporary authors. Now in her late seventies, she is still
writing, and her latest novel *Transit* reveals how abreast of
the times she is with respect to problems that beset late
twentieth-century society.

Haasse was born in Batavia (Jakarta) in the Dutch East
Indies on 2 February 1918. She spent her childhood and
teen years in a completely Dutch milieu, outside the world
of the Indonesians and the Indo-Europeans. Her mother
was an accomplished pianist, and her father, Chief Inspector
of Finances for the Dutch colonial government, was an
avid reader and the possessor of a well-stocked library. As a
child, she devoured the historical novels in her father's collection, and early in her life she herself began to write.

In Holland she studied Scandinavian languages at the
University of Amsterdam and also attended the Amsterdam
School of Drama. Her interest in history and literature and
the many historical novels she produced led to an honorary
doctorate received in 1988 from the University of Utrecht;
and at the University of Groningen her novel about the
life of Charles of Orleans is required reading for history
students as an introduction to the fifteenth century. She
says that her fascination with history is not her only

motivation for writing: she discovers, sometimes much later, that she has chosen certain characters in her novels in order to express herself through them.

'Forever a Stranger' or 'Oeroeg', as the book was known in the original Dutch edition, was the result of her desire to express certain emotions related to the Dutch East Indies and Indonesia. She writes of this, her very first novel:

In 1938 I left the Indies to study in The Netherlands. The war and the ensuing Indonesian struggle for independence represented for me the definitive leave-taking from the country that I considered my 'ouderlijk huis', my 'childhood home'. When the so-called 'police actions' of the Dutch began in 1947 I suddenly realized that I no longer belonged there, that the country that I had so naturally loved as a child did not desire my presence. I also realized that I had previously had little understanding of the situation and that I did not really know the country and its people. The friendship in the book between the Dutch 'I' and the Indonesian boy Oeroeg is actually the personification of my love for the Indies and the inevitable end of the relationship with the country that I had had as a child.

'Forever a Stranger', however, is no historical document. The military operations of the Dutch were just beginning when Haasse wrote her novel. When the book was later filmed (and entered in the 1993 Cannes Film Festival), the scenario began where the book ended.

On the surface, 'Forever a Stranger' is the story of two boys, one Dutch, one Indonesian, who grow up together in close companionship in spite of the differences in their race and social class. The Dutch boy is the son of the administrator of a tea plantation in the mountains of West

Java, and the Indonesian Oeroeg is the son of a Sundanese (West Javanese) plantation foreman. Later, after the Indonesian becomes aware of his inferior social position in the Dutch colony, he becomes a nationalist and the two friends become estranged. After the Second World War and the Indonesian revolution, when the young Dutchman, now an engineer from the University of Delft, returns to the country of his birth to work there, he meets, or thinks he meets, his old friend again, but now in a confrontation between Indonesian revolutionary and Dutch adversary. A close human relationship has been destroyed by colonialism, war, revolution.

Haasse's explanation of the story is different, however. At the end of the book, the Dutch protagonist says:

... and Oeroeg—I shall never meet him again. It is superfluous to admit that I did not understand him. I knew him as I knew Telaga Hideung—as the sparkling surface of a crater lake. But I never fathomed the depths. Is it too late? Am I forever to be a stranger in the land of my birth, on the earth from which I do not wish to be transplanted? Only time will tell.

Haasse is speaking through him to express her own feelings about the Dutch East Indies and Indonesia. In one of her autobiographies, she writes, 'I was born in the Indies, and yet I have perhaps never been anything more than a foreigner there.'

To this day there is a debate in The Netherlands about whether the aforementioned 'police actions', the military operations undertaken by the Dutch to regain the colony they had 'lost' during the Japanese Occupation were right or wrong. It was just at the beginning of these operations that 'Forever a Stranger' appeared, and it was given an extraordinary reception, perhaps because it was considered so timely. It was even unanimously chosen from nineteen anonymous manuscripts submitted for the Netherlands Book Week in 1948. In later discussions of the book related to the subject of Dutch colonial policy, it was said that, like Haasse herself, the Dutch had not really known and understood the Indonesian people, had not 'fathomed the depths' of their feelings and aspirations.

Haasse's other books about Indonesia include a description of a trip through Java when she returned to the country after an absence of thirty years; a number of autobiographical works; and *Heren van de Thee* [The Tea Barons], a historical novel about the extended family of Rudolf Kerkhoven and their lives on a tea and quinine plantation in the mountainous region of West Java known as the Priangan.

The other two stories in this book also show how receptive Haasse was to impressions absorbed into her memory and imagination as a child and young girl. The background for the story of the Japanese family and their Indo-European neighbours in 'Lidah Boeaja (Crocodile's Tongue)' is her recollection of solitary wanderings through remote neighbourhoods during the quiet hours of the Indies 'siesta'. The inspiration for the story 'An Affair (Egbert's Story)' was an actual event, a suicide, told in whispers by a friend of her mother's while she herself pretended to be absorbed in a book, paying no attention to their conversation.

It is the Indonesian landscape, however, that has influenced her most. The vast expanse of tea plantations and rice fields in all shades of green, against the mountain ranges in the background, has always remained with her and informed her writing. She says, 'Perhaps this is why I like to write about history. I am always in search of open spaces, of the unbounded. If this spaciousness is not available geographically, I search for it in time.'

A Note on Spelling

THE spelling of Indonesian words was changed in 1972. Wherever the author has used the 'old' spelling, it has been retained.

The main differences between the two orthographies are as follows:

Old Spelling	New Spelling
tj [tʃ]	c
j [j]	y
dj [dʒ]	j
ch [k]	kh
nj [ny]	ny
sj [ʃ]	sy
oe [u:]	u

Forever a Stranger

Kebon Djati

OEROEG was my friend. When I think back to my childhood and the years when I was growing up, the picture of
Oeroeg invariably appears to me as though my memory is
like one of those magic pictures we used to buy, three for
ten cents: shiny yellowish things with paper pasted over
them that you had to scratch over with a pencil until the
hidden picture appeared. That is how Oeroeg comes back
to me when I let myself delve deeply into the past. Although the surroundings are different, depending on
whether the period I recall is a shorter or longer time ago,
I always see Oeroeg, on the dilapidated Kebon Djati plantation, or in the brownish-red trodden-down mud of the
paths through the rice fields, deep in the mountains of the
Priangan; in the hot carriages of the little train that carried
us back and forth to the elementary school in Soekaboemi,
and later, at the boarding-school in Batavia, when both of
us were in secondary school. Oeroeg and I, playing, and
going on hunting expeditions in the wilderness—Oeroeg
and I, huddled over our homework, over stamp collections
and forbidden books—Oeroeg and I, always together, in
all stages of our development from boyhood to manhood.

I think I can say that Oeroeg has been burnt into my life, like a seal, a brand: more than ever at the moment, now that every contact, every meeting, belongs for good to the past. I do not know why I want to be fully alive to my relationship with Oeroeg, to everything that he meant, and still means to me. Maybe what provokes me is his irrevocable, incomprehensible differentness; that secret of spirit and blood that raised no problem in our youth and childhood but that now seems more tormenting than ever.

Oeroeg was the eldest son of my father's *mandoer* (foreman), and, like me, was born on the Kebon Djati plantation where my father was administrator. There was only a few weeks' difference in our ages. My mother was very fond of Oeroeg's mother, probably because, as a young Dutch woman in the Indies for the first time, and on remote Kebon Djati hidden away from any contact with friends of the same race and sex, she found understanding and devotion in the gentle, cheerful Sidris. The tie was all the stronger since they were both experiencing their first pregnancy. In the long, long hours of the day, when my father was making his inspection tours of the plantation, or working in his office beside the factory, my mother and Sidris would sit on the back veranda with their needlework, and in a confidential game of question and answer, talk about their experiences, their fears, and desires, the innumerable nuances in moods and emotions that only find an echo from woman to woman. They saw things differently, and only spoke each other's language falteringly, but under the peignoir and under the sarong, the same miracle was swelling in both their wombs. And so it was no wonder that later those hours together continued, that I, bedded in rattan and tulle, slept next to my mother's chair, and Oeroeg swung happily in the batik *selendang* (shawl) on Sidris's back. The earliest picture that I can recall to memory shows the two women between the marble columns of the back veranda, surrounded by piles of white cloth for mending. Oeroeg and I, in striped playsuits, crawled about among the pots of ferns that bordered the steps of the veranda. All around us were bright, brilliantly coloured spots—red, yellow, and orange—that swayed to and fro in the wind; in later years I knew that these were cannas planted closely together in the backyard. Oeroeg and I poked about in the gravel looking for the little, more or less transparent pebbles that the Indonesians polished till they resembled semi-precious stones. The air was full of the buzzing of insects, and wood-pigeons cooed in their bamboo cages that had been hoisted up behind the servants' quarters. A dog barked, cackling chickens dashed over the yard, and water gushed from the well. The wind from the mountains was cool, and carried along with it the smell of smoke from the villages further up. My mother poured out vanilla syrup for us in coloured glasses—red for me, green for Oeroeg. The ice tinkled against the sides. I never get a whiff of vanilla without this image reappearing in my consciousness—Oeroeg and I, all our attention on our syrup on the steps with little stones scattered over them, the waving of ferns and flowers in the wind, and all the sounds of the morning in the sunny yard.

Two years after my birth, my mother had a miscarriage, and thereafter she never became pregnant again. Perhaps that was the reason Oeroeg was always my only playmate, though Sidris had one child after another. Those hours on the back veranda came to an end. Sometimes my mother would sit there alone, writing letters or sewing, but more often I would find her in the dim light of her bedroom, reclining in a cane lounge-chair, with a wet cloth on her forehead. I always found something to do with Oeroeg, wandering over the grounds or outside the fence, in the kampong and in the adjacent parts of the tea plantation. And I often spent whole days in the house of the *mandoer*, with Sidris and Oeroeg's brothers and sisters. They lived in the only stone house in the kampong. Their yard bordered on the river, which at this part was narrow and full of large stones. We children jumped from stone to stone or waded through the spots where the shallow, crystal-clear water lay as still as in a basin, as we searched for red and greenish-yellow crabs, dragonflies, and other creatures. Above the pools, under the dense scrub along the bank, were swarms of insects. While the smaller children, naked and motionless, squatted in the light-brown mud, Oeroeg and I rooted about with sticks in the shadowy hiding places under the low-hanging green.

We were then both about six years old. I was taller, but Oeroeg, with his slender muscular body, looked older. The line running from his shoulder-blades down to his narrow, somewhat flattened hips, already had the same nonchalant suppleness that could be observed in the half-grown boys and young men who worked in the factory and in the rice paddies. Huddled up, with his pliant toes bent under, he balanced himself on stones and tree branches, surer of his position than I, and reacting more quickly when he lost his balance. At that time I was so absorbed in our games that I was scarcely conscious of these things. I did hate my freckles and was annoyed when my skin turned red and peeled in the fierce heat of the sun, and I was envious of Oeroeg's dark even colour, only here and there disfigured by the pink spots that indicated a previously suffered skin disease. Oeroeg's face was flat and broad like his mother Sidris's, but without the feature of gentle cheerfulness that made her so attractive. As far back as I can remember, that tense, searching look, as though he was waiting for a sound, a signal, that no one could hear but himself, never left his eyes. Oeroeg's eyes were so dark that even the whites seemed shaded. When he was happy, and when he was angry too, he would press his eyes together slightly, so that the sparkle in them was hidden under the wreath of his short, stiff eyelashes. Oeroeg never laughed with his mouth wide open, like most Indonesians. In a burst of genuine irrepressible mirth, he would sit rocking silently back and forth, his face distorted into a grimace. Usually, the way we enjoyed things was not the same. If I leaped over the stones in the river shouting for joy and excitement after an extraordinarily successful catch—a crab, marbled pink like a shell, or a transparent salamander—Oeroeg only stared at the prize with a tense, dark look and evenly dilated nostrils. He had a way with animals, catching and carrying them without ever sustaining any injury. I preferred keeping them in boxes and cans covered with glass. My mother—in spite of an abhorrence of 'animals' that she had never been able to conquer—had given me permission to keep my collection in one of the outbuildings. But Oeroeg took little pleasure in the regular care and maintenance of this menagerie. His attention slackened where mine began. He liked to tease a crab with a straw, until the animal braced itself in a position of attack. He amused himself most by having two different kinds of animals fight against each other—he brought toads to measure their strength against river- and land-crabs, incited bird-eating spiders against salamanders, wasps against dragonflies. Perhaps it would be going too far to call this cruelty. Oeroeg was not cruel; only he did not have the feeling that makes a Westerner often want to save and respect an animal out of a half-conscious sense of related-ness. When I, the spectator of these gladiatorial battles, cried out, overcome partly by excitement, and partly by a feeling of guilt and horror, Oeroeg gave me a sidelong glance of surprise and said, in Sundanese, as though to soothe me, 'It doesn't matter—they're only animals.' But what we liked best of all our games was pretending that we were hunters and explorers, prowling through the fruit-trees in the backyard, or what was more exciting, on the stones in the river.

When my father was away on a tour of duty and my mother was suffering from one of her ever more frequently recurring headaches, I had my lunch at Oeroeg's house. Sidris, ageing quickly and somewhat shapeless after having borne so many children, squatted at the back of her house among the kitchen utensils with a number of female rel-atives, frying pancakes filled with rice and meat in hot oil. The children sat all around and silently dispatched what Sidris presented to them on banana leaves. Skinny chickens picked at the spilled grains of rice, and a black dog, always mangy, stole about at a distance, waiting until we went away. I felt at home at Oeroeg's, inside the house as well, where it smelled of the coconut oil that Sidris rubbed into her hair-knot. On the front porch stood a few deep old rocking chairs, gifts from my mother. Paper fans and coloured pictures out of magazines were pinned to the white walls of woven bamboo. What I liked best was a curtain of Japanese beads that camouflaged the opening to the two bedrooms. It represented the Fujiyama, an unreal turquoise blue mountain with bright red and sea-green blossoming trees in the foreground. As we walked through the screen, the beaded strings closed behind us, rustling mysteriously. Day after day, Oeroeg's grandfather sat on one of the rocking chairs, in striped cotton pyjamas with a sarong thrown loosely over his shoulders. He was in his dotage, and did nothing but nod his head and laugh, showing the stumps of his teeth, coloured dark red from chewing *sirih* (betel-nut). In front of the house there was a small yard, separated from the rest of the kampong by a low whitewashed wall. In the reddish earth, Oeroeg and I, following the example of the gardener at my house, had laid out flower-beds, not from identical white stones and decorative flower pots, but from bottles whose necks we had buried in the ground, so that only the shining dark green concave bottoms stood up out of the soil. No grass grew in Sidris's garden, nor trees either, but our flower-beds were none the less effective.

Sometimes Oeroeg came to my house, but neither one of us enjoyed these visits. Wild games were out of the question because of my mother, and we were too restless to play with building blocks or look at pictures. During the rainy season, when the garden had been transformed into a swamp and the paths into mountain streams, we sat on the steps of the back veranda, stretching our toes out into the spray of drops thrown up by the water gushing down from the roof overhang. Streams poured out of the rain-spouts into the ditches and the well in a monotonous minor key, frogs croaked all the day long, and no other sound could be heard under the low leaden-grey skies that hid the mountain tops from us.

During the rainy season, my father was more frequently at home. He sat in the inner veranda that served as his study, occasionally with my mother, but mostly alone. Oeroeg and I were given food by the *baboe* (female domestic servant) at a separate table, at a different time from when my parents had their meals. In the evenings, I would sometimes have dinner with my father and mother, but on these occasions I never felt comfortable. Under the low-hanging lamp, the table was like an island of loneliness in the immense back gallery. Now and then my parents exchanged a few words in subdued voices, mostly about household affairs, the factory, matters relating to the employees. The *djongos* (male servant) moved silently back and forth between the table and the pantry to serve us, his head-cloth freshly folded like a crown. When he bowed low beside me, I smelled the mixed scent of sweet tobacco and starch, forever confined in his sarong and white jacket.

Sometimes my father asked me questions: whether I had been a good boy, what I had been doing all day. I could never reply to these questions openly, since I knew that my answers would result in a quarrel between my parents. My father listened to my somewhat faltering reports of our games and adventures with a frown of displeasure between his eyebrows.

'The boy should not be in the kampong,' he usually said, as I fell silent. 'It's bad for him. He can't speak one decent word of Dutch. Don't you know that? He's turning into the veriest *kacung* (native boy). Why don't you keep him at home?'

'He has to go to school,' my mother said once, in response to such a tirade. 'He's six years old now. How can I keep him in the house? He has to be kept busy. He has to play. There are no other children here. He's always alone.'

'Oeroeg!' I burst out, indignant that she neglected to mention my best, in fact, my only friend. My mother shrugged.

'He won't be accepted at any school with the language he speaks,' continued my father. 'Every other word is Sundanese. First of all, he has to learn to open his mouth respectably in Dutch!'

I did not witness further discussions, but one afternoon, a few days later, a young employee from the factory, who, I heard later, had originally studied to be a teacher, came to the house. It was made clear to me that I would be prepared full steam to enter the elementary school in Soekaboemi. In despair, I put up a stubborn resistance. Outside, in the yard, Oeroeg was waiting for me. My mother had sent him away when my new teacher arrived. I saw Oeroeg's bright-red shirt among the shrubs that hid the servant's quarters from view. We had made a plan to dig up ant-lions. While my mother was talking to the young man, I tried in vain to slip away over the back veranda. I had to sit on a chair and answer questions without lapsing into Sundanese, which I knew much better than Dutch. Oeroeg came as far as the steps of the back veranda, where he looked inside in silence and amazement. He stood there, motionless, until the end of the 'lesson'.

* * *

That evening, my mother came to my room before I went to sleep, something she rarely did. While I washed myself and undressed under the supervision of the *baboe*, she told me that the hours with Mijnheer Bollinger would be continued until August, the month the schools started. I said that I did not want to go to school, thinking of having to sit still and answer questions. My mother enumerated all the pleasures of my future state, but the prospect of learning to read, write, and do arithmetic did not appeal to me at all.

'Is Oeroeg going along?' I asked when she had had her say. My mother sighed. She was sitting on a low cane chair beside the bed in a kimono of flowered material, surrounded by her inseparable scent of eau de cologne.

'What a question!' she exclaimed impatiently, patting her temples with a damp handkerchief. 'Don't be so stupid. Oeroeg is a native, isn't he?'

'Doesn't *he* have to go to school?' I persisted. My mother stood up and gave me a perfunctory kiss on the cheek.

'Maybe,' she said vaguely. 'To another kind of school, of course. Now go to sleep.'

I climbed into my bed, and the *baboe* tucked in the *klamboe* (mosquito net).

'I'm going to ask Sidris,' I began, squatting at the foot of the bed while I looked at my mother through the mesh of the *klamboe*. She remained standing by the door.

'You may not play in the kampong any more,' she said, in that irritable, nervous tone that announced an approaching headache. 'Your father doesn't want you to. Let Oeroeg come here if you like. Good night.'

And so it came to pass. Although, especially in the absence of my father, I often saw a chance to escape to the river and to Sidris's hospitable home, most of the time, Oeroeg came to my house to play. We plundered the fruit-trees in the garden, continued to hunt for all sorts of beasts among the bushes in the neglected backyard, or in rainy weather, squatted between the columns of the veranda doing things that I can no longer remember. When Mijnheer Bollinger came for the 'lesson', Oeroeg remained nearby. He sat on the floor some distance away from us and watched us intently. He had accepted the news that I was going to school fairly calmly. He only asked if I would go by train, and when I replied in the affirmative, he had imitated the puffing and jolting of a locomotive with fanatic concentration. Not a single word was ever exchanged again about the school or about Mijnheer Bollinger. Oeroeg and I both regarded it as self-evident that he should be present during these lessons. My mother, who now and then walked in when Mijnheer Bollinger was there, made a few attempts to send Oeroeg away. He left, slowly, but within a quarter of an hour, he was standing there again among the flowerpots near the steps of the back veranda.

My father seemed satisfied with the progress I made in enlarging my vocabulary; but until far into my school years, I retained the strong accent of someone who could express himself more fluently in Sundanese than in Dutch. The months passed, and preparations were made for my entrance to school. An old native dressmaker sat behind the treadle sewing machine in the inner gallery and produced, under my mother's supervision, the trousers and shirts that would replace my cotton playsuits. A Chinese came to fit my sandals. Finally, my father returned from a tour of duty bringing a school-bag and all its contents. I showed myself to Oereog all decked out in my new school clothes. He looked at me most attentively, investigated the contents of my pencil-case, and asked again if I would travel by train every day.

* * *

One evening my mother walked through the house dressed up and neatly coiffured, which for her was very rare. The small lamps in the inner gallery had been lit and our *djongos* put dishes with snacks on the table. I heard that we were having guests: people from Batavia who were staying at a plantation in the neighbourhood, and Mijnheer Bollinger.

'No, you're not having a lesson,' said my mother, smiling, as she stood admiring herself in the mirror. 'If you behave yourself, you can have dinner with us.'

The *baboe* dressed me in one of my school uniforms. Quite impressed by this unusual state of affairs, I waited for the guests in front of the house. The sun had just set, and the trees that bordered the garden were silhouetted against the red cloud banks in the west. On the mountain tops it was still light. The soporific drone of insects could be heard in the darkness under shrubs and trees. In the kampong, they were beating on a hollow tree-trunk, as a sign that night had fallen. As I gazed at the fading glow above the horizon, I was overcome by a feeling of discomfort, an uneasy feeling I had never had before— I had to go to school; everything was going to change. I do not know if I was aware of it then; possibly I am searching now for an interpretation of the atmosphere then of melancholy and vague anxiety.

Down by the main road, a car turned into the gate, in a few moments stopping in front of the steps of the veranda. My mother appeared and greeted the guests. My father was among them. All I remember about the dinner was that my parents talked and laughed as never before, and that, in amazement at this, I nearly forgot to eat. After the *rijsttafel* (an Indonesian meal with rice and side dishes), when they had all gathered in the inner gallery—I was sitting unnoticed on the floor next to the gramophone cabinet—one of the guests suggested that they drive to Telaga Hideung, the Black Lake, that lay higher up in the mountains. My heart began to beat faster when I heard the name. In our fantasies, Oeroeg's and mine, the mountain lake played an important role, principally because of the mysterious stories that were circulated about it. Telaga Hideung, deep in the forest, was the meeting-place of evil spirits and souls of the dead; Neneh Kombel, a vampire in the form of an old woman who lay in wait for dead children, lived there.

One of the young women who lived in Sidris's house, a cousin of Oeroeg's named Satih, could tell the most frightening stories, all of them in some way connected with the Black Lake. In our imagination, we pictured it as a stretch of water, black as ink, where monsters and ghosts reigned supreme. Later, when we grew up, we would go there to battle against these creatures. Sometimes, when we were sitting together, tired of playing, or taking shelter from a shower, we would spin out this future gruesome expedition in detail, trembling with a fear that was yet pleasurable. As a very small child, I had once been to Telaga Hideung, but the only thing I remembered about the visit was my father in swimming trunks. The lake was used by employees of the plantation as a swimming pool, although not often, since it was too far away. Now Mijnheer Bollinger, pointing to the full moon that appeared as a reddish-orange disc behind the trees, proposed that they all go there for a swim. His plan met with general approval. When they were all standing, I crawled out of my hiding-place and pulled on my mother's dress. Her cheeks were flushed and her eyes were shining. I found her so strange that evening, quite lovely with her long ear-rings and her upswept hairdo.

'Aren't you in bed yet?' she asked, smiling absent-mindedly. 'Do you want to go along?'

My father, who was coming out of the bedroom with his arms full of swimming togs, frowned and raised objections, but the rest of the company, laughing and joking—there were a great many empty glasses on the table—persuaded him to let me go with them. I trembled with suspense. I was sorry that Oeroeg would not be with me, but on the other hand, I was full of pride and excitement that I would be the first to make the trip, even though it was under the protection of grown-ups, whose carefree gaity, as though it was for a pleasure trip, I secretly admired. The houseboy was sent to the *mandoer*'s house to get Deppoh, Oeroeg's father. I did not understand why, but did not dare to ask, nor to ask if Oeroeg could come along, for fear that at the last minute they would leave me behind. Finally, we were all in the car. I leaned against Mijnheer Bollinger's knees. On either side, on the running boards, stood Oeroeg's father and our gardener, Danoeh. We rode away. I looked at Deppoh, whom I did not know so well, and whom I held in almost as much awe as my own father. He was the handsomest Indonesian I had ever seen, tall and slender, with distinctively sharp features. He stood erect on the running board, holding on with only one hand. The moonlight shone on his white starched jacket. It seemed to me that he looked with disapproval upon the noisy group in the car. One of our guests told a long story that I did not understand at all, interrupted again and again by gales of laughter. My mother leaned back in the corner, between Mijnheer Bollinger and the side of the car, with her head against the folds of the open cap. I saw tears of laughter shining on her cheek. It was most uncomfortable standing against my teacher's knees, and I tried to find a place to sit on the edge of the seat, between him and my mother. As I pushed a part of my mother's dress to the side, I discovered that she was holding Mijnheer Bollinger's hand.

The night sky was a metallic blue. The moon was higher now, and had lost its red glow. The wind rustled in the grass and clumps of bamboo on either side of the road, which climbed high up the mountain slopes in wide curves. Now and then, we came to an open space that afforded a view of the plain below. The rice fields glistened white between black clusters of trees and here and there a vague flicker of light appeared in a village house. Viewed from above, the tea gardens with their long uniform rows of plants were like flocks of sheep disposed in an orderly fashion, motionless in the moonlight, and only at certain places shaded by the light foliage of albizzia trees.

As we rode further, we could hear the splash of falling water. Between the moss-covered stone of the steep mountain face sparkled little streams that, along the way, united to form a rivulet. The air was almost cold, and at this height there hung a smell of damp earth and rotting leaves. Around a curve in the road, the forest began, and we drove into the darkness amidst uproarious laughter and raillery. I squatted on the floor of the car, fearful of the dark all around, full of sounds of the night. Only the nearness of Deppoh, who stood immovable on the running board, gave me a feeling of security. It seemed to me that the others, with all their noise and frolicking, were not aware of this realm full of demons. But Deppoh knew. As I looked up at his sharply outlined profile, which I could make out whenever the moonlight succeeded in penetrating the roof of leaves above us, I was sure of it.

The car stopped and everyone climbed out. I pushed against Deppoh, who led the way through the low scrub with a pocket torch. We climbed a narrow stony path that led steeply upwards. All around there was a rustling, as though many invisible beings were stealing up the mountain with us. Something jumped above our heads through the branches.

'A flying squirrel,' said Deppoh, and as I held on tightly to his sarong, I whispered, still trembling with fear, 'Not Neneh Kombel?'

'Ah, no!' Deppoh's reply was abrupt, but decisive. 'The *sinyo besar* (young master) should have been in bed long ago.'

He stopped and then turned around, lighting the path with the torch so that the others could catch up with us. They climbed up in a row, one behind the other. My mother and Mijnheer Bollinger were last. We moved ahead as though we were passing though a dark tunnel in which only Deppoh's torch cast a beam of light. I walked beside him in silence and did my best not to let the noises in the undergrowth frighten me.

'Isn't Oeroeg going to school?' I finally asked. Just thinking of Oeroeg seemed to bring an element of reality into this black world of night.

'Maybe,' replied Deppoh.

There was a distant gleam, and when we came closer, I saw that it was moonlight streaming down through the openings in the foliage, creating a shaft of light.

'There is Telaga Hideung,' announced Deppoh calmly. My heart pounded, but retreat was now impossible. My father and two men I did not know began to run, betting on who would first reach the lake. I felt ashamed for them, and spied fearfully left and right at ghosts gliding past. From afar, I could hear the loud laughter of the racers. Now my mother, Mijnheer Bollinger, and another lady passed us. The gardener Danoeh walked silently on the other side of me, and we made our way through the moonlight to the bank of the lake. A feeling of disappointment crept over me. What I found was not the immense black expanse of water of my fantasies, but a pool, almost a pond, enclosed on all sides by mountain faces rising straight up, overgrown with dense forest. The feathery, woolly crowns of trees were a luminous pale blue in the moonlight, and the lake resembled the shining bottom of a vase shaped like a truncated cone. Water plants floated on the surface, especially along the banks. The leaves and the lianas of some of the trees hung over and into the water. The buzzing of the thousand-voiced insects and the cries of the night creatures of the forest filled the awesome silence. Above the tree-tops, the stars glittered with ice-cold light. I stared at the black edge of the lake on the other side, where the leaves touched the surface of the water, and it was easy for me to imagine that the evil spirits were hiding there, ready for the attack. When Deppoh and Danoeh walked a short distance into the darkness, I reluctantly chose the company of my mother and the others.

I now saw why Oeroeg's father and the gardener had come along. There was the sound of a soft splash in the water, and a raft on which a small two-storey bamboo house had been built moved closer along the shore, punted ahead by the two men. At a spot on the edge of the lake where it was least marshy, we climbed on to the raft, a floor of thin boards resting on hollow bamboo poles. While the women sat on an old cane bench and the men disappeared into the little house with their swimming trunks, the raft drifted slowly out to the middle of the lake. Danoeh walked back and forth poling the raft. Deppoh, in a muffled voice, gave instructions and made soundings from time to time, searching for a place suitable for swimming. My father and his guests laughed uproariously in the little bamboo house. I stood beside the bench on which the ladies were sitting and peered at the banks where every movement of the leaves with moonlight shining on them, every sound, seemed to be coming from some supernatural source. Swimming seemed to me to be a dangerous and absurd enterprise— hadn't Satih told us that the lake was thousands of metres deep and that it was inhabited by a giant snake? Without any plausible reason, circles formed on the surface and the moonlight gleamed in the ripples flowing out from them. Was there something moving there in the depths? I screamed with fear when just beside the raft something white emerged, and the jollity of the others only partially reassured me when it proved to be Mijnheer Bollinger, who had soundlessly slid into the water to frighten us. The bodies of the men glimmered white in the moonlight. They dived after each other and came up sneezing and spitting. The bowl in the centre of the mountains was suddenly full of resonating voices and splashing water. I could not understand how they could be so carefree.

Danoeh manœuvred the raft so as to make it continue drifting in the same spot. Deppoh squatted in the shadow of the bamboo house—I saw only the light from the tip of his cigarette glowing in the dark. His restful attitude had a somewhat calming effect on me. I went up to him and sat beside him.

'Is it true that Neneh Kombel eats children?' I asked in a whisper.

'Ah!' replied Deppoh with an undertone of impatience. He did not go any further into what I had said, but bent over and called out a warning to the men in the lake.

'Water plants,' he said to me, in explanation. 'The only place that's any good for swimming is around the raft. The water plants catch hold of you and won't let you go, and you drown. I know Telaga Hideung.'

I stared at the water in fascination, and wished that my father would come out, on to the safety of the raft. I did not have to wait long. The cold of approaching night forced the swimmers to leave the water. Sneezing, they stood trampling on the raft, drying themselves with their towels. Then, in a fit of silliness, they began to play leap-frog, following each other around the bench where the women were sitting. The floor boards creaked, the entire raft wobbled and shook. Deppoh cried, 'Watch out! The bamboo is old!' but no one paid any attention to him.

They had now started playing 'Jonah and the Whale', in which the victim is grabbed by both arms and legs and thrown into the water. They were going after Mijnheer Bollinger, who fled to the little house and climbed up on to the flat roof. My father and the two guests followed him as the women cheered them on. I found the chase exciting and walked around the house to the outer edge of the raft to find out how Mijnheer would escape. That was all I remembered. There was a sound of splitting bamboo, chaotic screaming all around, and I fell headlong into ice-cold darkness.

* * *

When I came to, I was lying in my own bed. Through the white mist of the *klamboe,* I saw a small light burning. My father was standing at the foot of the bed looking at me. I did not understand what could have happened. At first it seemed to me as though I had been dreaming of the lake in the moonlight, but my hair was wet, and there was a taste of muddy water in my mouth. I moved slightly and called out. My father opened the *klamboe* and now the *baboe* appeared behind him with a glass of steaming liquid in her hand. I drank it, leaning against my father. I went back to sleep immediately. It was not until days later that I heard how it had all happened. The raft, already overladen, had not been able to bear the strain of their game, in which they climbed up on to the bamboo house. The boards, half-decayed with age, had given way under the weight of the romping men. Top-heavy on one side, that part of the raft had broken up, capsized, and disappeared in the water. Although all the members of the party were shocked and had injuries from splinters of bamboo and sharp pieces of wood, they all came to the surface at once. I was the only one missing. Deppoh dived under for me, among the wreckage and the wickerwork. Not long afterwards, my father found me, half-choked, entangled in the torn bamboo wall of the house. The party had arrived at the shore on the part of the raft that was still whole.

'And ... Deppoh?' I asked, my heart beating with the foreboding of something terrible.

'Deppoh was caught in the water plants,' said my father, slowly and gently, as though he hoped that I would not hear it. 'Deppoh is dead.'

*   *   *

No greater disaster could have befallen me. What weighed most heavily upon me was the realization that Deppoh had lost his life looking for me. I could not shake off the thought of the water plants that he had told me about that evening at the lake. At all hours of the day and night, I was oppressed by the horrible vision of his body, struggling among the tough, viscous stems. Again and again, I woke up screaming. I was feverishly aware of shapes beside my bed: my mother, Mijnheer Bollinger with a bandage around his head, my father. Once Oeroeg came, but we barely exchanged a word. Oeroeg was unnaturally quiet and shy in the presence of adults, and he was awed by my illness and the dimly lit bedroom. I was tormented by the idea that I was the cause of his father's death. We stared at each other in silence.

'Oeroeg has come to say goodbye,' my mother said. 'He's going to move away.'

And then I was told what was going to happen. A new *mandoer* was going to move into the stone house on the river; Sidris and the children would live with a relative in one of the villages higher up the mountain.

I have never found out what finally caused the turn of the scale: my desperate sadness at the prospect of being separated from Oeroeg, my parents' feeling of guilt with respect to Deppoh's son, or perhaps the motherly concern and ambition of the humble and modest Sidris. One day, for the first time since my early childhood, she came to our house again, immaculately dressed, with a fragrant flower in her hair-knot, her forehead coated with powder. She was with my mother for a long time; I heard their voices in the bedroom, which adjoined mine, but I could not understand a word. What was decided there had far-reaching consequences. Oeroeg was to come and live with our houseboy, who was a grandnephew of Deppoh's, and he would attend the Dutch Primary School for Native Indonesians in Soekaboemi.

*   *   *

As I now look back on our primary school years, the days of all those years seem to flow together in one image, probably because the same impressions followed one upon another so regularly and unchangingly. Early every morning, we rode in the car to the station, a half-hour's drive from the plantation. Grass and leaves glistened in heavy dew, the sun had barely risen, and the blue haze of the morning lay over the land. Indonesians were carrying fruit and other wares to the station to catch the train on time, bent under the burden of their *pikolan* (carrying poles). They moved slowly and rhythmically over the road. A farmer drove his buffaloes on to the rice field, assisted by small boys uttering shrill cries as they kept the animals on the grassy ridges. Oeroeg knew some of them, and hanging out of the car, screamed a greeting. From the other direction came, in groups, the tea pickers and plantation workers. The women looked around at us, laughing under the folds of the *slendang* they wore wound about their heads. Small children, dogs, and chickens ran out of the village houses, hidden under the shade of tall trees.

At the station, there was always the same hustle and bustle. There were piles of baskets and crowds of people waiting for the first train; there was a *warung* that provided an opportunity for an early meal. Often Oeroeg and I succumbed to the temptation of a portion of *roedjak*, unripe fruit served with a hot sauce, which we hastily lapped up out of a folded leaf. Then the train came in: the tiny mountain locomotive with its tow of windowless carriages furnished with long wooden benches. Although Oeroeg and I were allowed to travel second-class, we chose the crowded carriages, where we were often offered a piece of fruit or some nuts and where there was always something to be seen or heard. I know every stone, every telegraph pole, every bridge of that passage through the mountains of the Priangan. I would be able to draw with my eyes closed the landscape on either side of the windows: the sloping terraces of the rice paddies, the wooded cone-shaped hills which further up became blue mountain ridges, the small shelters on the field, the village houses among clumps of bamboo, an occasional station, plastered white, where groups of marketers were waiting with their wares. When we arrived in Soekaboemi, the sun was already beating down and the world was divided into brilliant light and cool shade. We walked a short distance through the city—to us Soekaboemi was a city—and then our ways parted: Oeroeg went to his school, I to mine.

There was little difference in the subjects we were given to study, only Oeroeg had Dutch as an extra subject. The hours we spent in our classrooms must have been very much the same: the never-ending hum of the voices of children droning a lesson in chorus, and the accompanying sound of shuffling feet, the scratch of slate-pencils and pens, while outside the trees rustled in the breeze, and the hot air vibrated above the asphalt of the street. At one o'clock, we saw each other again at a spot where we had agreed to meet. When I ran to it, there was Oeroeg standing in the shade of a tree, barefoot, but otherwise, I thought, well-dressed in velvet trousers with a boy scout belt, and with the *pici*, the black cap of the Muslim boys, on his head. We often bought, for a few cents, brightly coloured ice lollipops, frozen around thin pieces of wood, so that you could suck them off, or in the train we treated ourselves to a highly sticky delicacy, a kind of coconut pudding. At this time of day, it was extremely hot, even in the higher region of Kebon Djati, and the first thing we did when we arrived home was to cool ourselves off. I went to the bathroom and Oeroeg to the well behind the outbuildings.

Although in the afternoon hours we still occupied ourselves with our old games in the garden and by the river, we gradually began to be interested in other things. We collected stamps, cigar bands, and pictures of cars and planes. Oeroeg was enthralled by planes. His imitation of the screech of a plane landing was thoroughly realistic. With his arms stretched out wide, he ran around in circles, jumped, squatted, and crept, and finally, making a series of sounds that were supposed to represent a crash, fell on the ground. I was never able to do this. A sort of shyness, perhaps embarrassment, or powerlessness to give myself up so completely to play prevented me from enjoying myself fully in screams and gestures as Oeroeg could. At that time, I also discovered the joy of reading—an activity that appealed to Oeroeg only moderately, at the most if there were pictures in the books. He excelled in drawing, showing a strong preference for the symmetrical figures of the examples from school, circles and triangles ingeniously drawn through and about each other and coloured with striking tints.

Since I took the presence of Oeroeg for granted, I did not have a clear idea of the peculiar position that Oeroeg held with us, in the middle between housemate and subordinate. He ate and slept in the servants' rooms, but spent the greater part of the day with me. My mother calmly let this take its own course—it was not until much later that I realized that the friendship between Oeroeg and me meant a relief for her. She was less solitary than before and had bought a horse, on which she rode through the tea gardens, often in the · company of Mijnheer Bollinger. My father was busy and often away on trips. On holidays Oeroeg went to visit Sidris, and I usually went along. Sidris now lived with her children in a small house in the village which seemed to me unbelievably neglected and dirty in contrast to the old house on the river. Oeroeg's grandfather had died, and the rocking chairs had disappeared with him. Only the Japanese beaded screen recalled past glory. The young children, in dirty and torn clothing, crowded around Oeroeg and me when we came, full of awe and admiration, but too shy to ask any questions. On these occasions Oeroeg needed no encouragement. Surrounded by relatives and interested villagers who had come to the house, he talked about the train, about Soekaboemi, about the lessons at school. Sidris, whose face and figure were more clearly showing traces of ageing, listened to her son with pleasure and satisfaction. From time to time, she interrupted him with short exclamations or with a variety of tongue clackings which could express the most diverse feelings. Oeroeg's cousin Satih, who had continued living with Sidris, used these story hours to take one of the younger children between her knees and delouse it. Satih was a pretty girl of about sixteen, almost too plump in her faded *kebaya* (Indonesian woman's blouse).

I never had the feeling of being an outsider among these people; on the contrary. Even in the dilapidated village house, on a muddy piece of land, I felt more at home than in the hollow dimly lighted rooms of our house. After such a visit, when, with Oeroeg, I descended the stony path to the plantation, it seemed as though I had said goodbye to my own family, As for Oeroeg and myself, there was never any doubt in my mind that we were completely equal. Although with respect to the houseboy, the *baboe*, and Danoeh, I was perhaps half-aware of a differ-. ence in race and station, Oeroeg's existence and mine had grown together to such a degree that I never felt this difference with regard to him. I was therefore the more surprised when I first noticed that Oeroeg's relationship with me and my parents evoked the ridicule and resistance of our servants. In the beginning, this was expressed in little things: teasing directed at 'Mijnheer' Oeroeg, sniggering among themselves, a word or gesture, but gradually their criticism was more strongly demonstrated by more or less open sabotage in the performance of the work they had been instructed to do. I knew now too that my father was paying for Oeroeg's schooling, and considering Deppoh's death, I found this only natural. What Oeroeg thought about this situation remained obscure. He was always the same, and walked in and out of our house as well as the outbuildings without a semblance of constraint.

I cannot imagine how lonely my childhood would have been if Oeroeg had not been there. In this case, I probably would have felt the divorce of my parents as a far greater blow. Because my mother, since my earliest years, had left me almost exclusively to the *baboe*, to Sidris and her family, and to Oeroeg, she was really no more than a stranger to me. The period of solitariness and migraine attacks was followed, after the disastrous evening at Telaga Hideung, by a time of restlessness and almost feverish activity. She went horseback riding; she went on long walks; she went shopping in Soekaboemi. For days on end, the old *djait* (seamstress) set the sewing-machine needle dancing on new materials, while my mother wandered nervously through the house, only occasionally sitting down to tear up letters or to play a game of patience. A few times we had guests, but it was usually Mijnheer Bollinger who kept my mother company, at tea, in the afternoons and evenings, or in walks around the plantation. Little by little, I had noticed the increasing chill in my parents' relationship, which had never been particularly close. Sometimes, when I lay in bed at night, I heard the slamming of doors and the sound of heated voices. Once I found my mother sobbing in the garden, where she said she had gone to feed the pigeons. Shortly thereafter, Mijnheer Bollinger left for Europe. It was not until much later that I understood the connection between all these details that at the time were so confusing and irrelevant to me.

When my father finally told me that my mother was going away on a journey for an indefinite period of time, I accepted this fact, incomprehensible as it was, merely as one of those things that as a child you apparently had to resign yourself to; but Oeroeg seemed secretly amused when I told him, and made a remark that I did not understand. Later, it became clear to me that the servants had their eyes all around them and that Oeroeg, through them, was well aware of what was going on in our house. He never mentioned it to me, not later either, when we were much older and such subjects were discussed. The only thing I ever noticed was a mocking and disdainful expression on his face whenever my mother's name was mentioned.

My mother's departure was marked by nervous activity. The inner gallery was full of luggage and packing-cases in which a large part of our household furnishings and linens were packed. During that time, my father remained invisible. Finally, one morning a car drove up, followed by one of the factory trucks on which the luggage was loaded. The tears and embraces of my mother, who had never been generous with signs of affection, threw me so out of balance that I cried desperately when the car rode away. For the occasion of her departure, I had been allowed to stay home from school for one day; but Oeroeg had gone to Soekaboemi as usual. I walked through the empty house, which, stripped now of paintings, vases, and cloths, was even chillier than otherwise. In the inner gallery, the chairs had been pushed back to make room for all the packing-cases. Straw and wood-wool were scattered over the floor. While I stood there, my father came home—he had withdrawn to the factory at the time I took leave of my mother. He sat on one of the chairs, sighed, and wiped the perspiration from his face and neck. For the first time in my life, I saw in him something other than only the administrator, the stern judge, the absolute ruler of my life as a child. I saw that his hair was thinning and that he was anxious and tired. I went up to him.

'So,' said my father evenly. 'Are you here? Big change, isn't it? Tell the boy to clean up this mess.'

He patted me absent-mindedly on my shoulder. 'Go out and play now,' he continued, and when I hesitated, he added, 'I was going to take you into the gardens this afternoon, but I'm having a visitor in the factory.'

'When Oeroeg comes home, we're going fishing,' I said hastily, to put his mind at ease. My father frowned a moment, and sighed again. Then, getting up and going to the bedroom, he said, 'Good. Good. Just go play with Oeroeg.'

And so a new phase in our lives began. I was then in the fourth grade of primary school.

* * *

One of the great events of those years for us was the arrival of Gerard Stokman, the employee who was to replace Mijnheer Bollinger. He was an exceptionally tall young man, thin, with a face that looked as though it had been chiselled out of shiny beige-coloured wood. He made his entrance on the plantation in a khaki suit with short trousers. The feet at the ends of his bony hairy legs were encased in gym shoes. His luggage, except for a few suit-cases, consisted for the most part of hunting equipment: guns, small-bore rifles, chopping-knives, poles mounted with iron, fish-nets and fishing rods, stained and dishev-elled game-bags, a tent, and all sorts of camping gear packed in canvas bags. Then stuffed animals and treated skins appeared, in crates the trucks had brought. Breathless, Oeroeg and I watched the unloading of this highly inter-esting baggage. Gerard Stokman lived in a small annexe not far from the house of the administrator. After all his possessions had been carried into his house, he sent the coolies away and began to unpack. He apparently consid-ered the presence of Oeroeg and me the most natural thing in the world. He let us take part in the storing and arranging of his belongings. He asked our advice on where to hang his collection of *Dayak* weapons. These, with their sharp teeth and barbed hooks, mightily goaded Oeroeg's imagination. With one of the assegais in his hand, he stalked imaginary enemies to the furthest corners of the annexe, playing the part in turn of the hunter and the hunted. I sat on my heels among the stuffed animals with their glass eyes and their wide-open mouths, varnished red inside. There were a monkey, a small panther, a flying squirrel, an alligator, birds, lizards, and a glass box full of treated snakes. In jam jars filled with a yellowish liquid and bound up with parchment paper floated indefinable parts of animals, pieces of skin, and what not. The owner of all these delicacies stood on a stool, and nailed the skin of an anteater to the wall. He answered our questions untiringly and told us all about himself. He was the son of an officer from Bandung, and he had lost his heart to Java, the hunt, and the outdoors. He was at loggerheads with his parents, since they objected to the profession he had chosen. He was quite philosophical about all this.

'It will turn out all right, or it will not turn out all right,' he said. 'But that is Verse Two. I need space around me. I'm not a person for an office or a barracks, and I have no desire to go to Holland. I've been to Holland—I went there when my father was on leave; and that was enough for me. This is a wonderful place. Did you boys know that it's full of wild boars up there? Saturday, if I have the chance, I'm going up into the mountains!'

Chances there were—plenty of them. No weekend passed without our seeing Gerard, as we called him almost immediately, take the path that led through the tea gardens into the forest, armed with rifle and chopping-knife, and followed by a coolie carrying a tent and provisions. These expeditions caused us intense excitement. Usually, we spent the evenings in Gerard's house listening to his stories, while he, chewing on his pipe, tended and polished his gun and treated the parts of his trophies of the hunt. The head of a pig was buried in the ground, a cleaning job for the ants. Oeroeg and I were engrossed in making guesses about the length of this process, and after a few weeks wanted to dig up the head to see how things were going. Gerard, however, strongly advised us to wait another month, and sure enough, at the end of this interval, the skull, nearly white, but not exactly sweet-smelling, made its appearance. It was cleaned again and brushed with colourless varnish; and then Gerard gave it to Oeroeg and me as a gift. It was our most precious possession. We took turns letting it stand beside our beds, and from time to time, we took it along to school to dazzle our classmates. But this was nothing compared to the radiance that surrounded us when Gerard decided to take us along on his weekly trips.

With a chopping-knife in our belts and a blanket tied on our backs, we climbed up behind our leader along the steep, stony forest paths. The enormous crowns of the trees far above our heads, woven into a perpetual green roof, allowed the penetration of only a small bit of daylight, so that we moved forward as though in the dim light of an aquarium. Under the trees, there hung a sharp smell of damp leaves, of layers of plants that were slowly decomposing to become solid earth. Clear, ice-cold water murmured among the scrub, in tiny streams of a hands' breadth, or as rivulets in a bed full of rounded grey stones. There was the constant sound of water falling and the air seemed saturated with fine droplets. There was something threatening in the silence under this immense dome of green, and in the beginning Oeroeg and I were afraid to speak other than in subdued voices. It seemed to us that there were many things in the shadowy depths of over-grown fissures, in the trunks twisted and scorched by lightning, to fill us with fear and trembling; but the thin figure of Gerard ahead inspired us with boundless trust.

On the saddle between two mountain peaks, he had discovered an old cabin which he had elevated to hunting lodge. This residence owed its fantastic exterior to the re-pairs Gerard had brought about. Lids of biscuit tins, pieces of wood in the greatest variety of shapes and colours, and primitive wickerwork of aerial roots cut down in the forest plugged the holes in the roof and the wall. A wall that was threatening to collapse was propped up by a neat pile of stones. The interior of the cabin consisted of two built-in sleeping bunks that Gerard called 'the rabbit hutches', a wobbly table, and a few stumps of tree-trunks to serve as chairs. A row of nails struck into the strongest part of the wall performed the function of a cupboard. On these we hung mugs, clothing, and weapons. From under one of the bunks Gerard took out a somewhat battered charcoal stove that he then placed on the blackened spot of earth under the roof in front of the cabin. Our cooking utensils were one pot and an empty margarine can. Ali, the coolie who always accompanied Gerard, collected dry wood, while Oeroeg and I drew water from the brook behind the cabin. With the help of an artificial waterfall and a piece of hollowed-out bamboo, Gerard had fabricated a water con-duit that was invaluable for all household activities. Even now, I can conjure up the vision, combined with the bitter smoky smell of burning wood, of those mealtimes in front of the cabin: Gerard sitting on a stump stirring the contents of a tin of corned beef through the rice; Ali, squatting with his arms hanging down over his knees spread wide apart; Oeroeg and I, barely able to sit still from excitement and hunger; and before us, past the bare stony slope of the mountain saddle, visible over the tops of the forest trees below, the descending highlands, in all shades of blue, grey, and green, with sharply delineated spots of shadow in the fissures and ravines; and still further below, all around, disappearing towards the horizon in a haze of heat, the plain over which the drifting clouds threw huge shadows.

In the afternoons, Gerard inspected the posts he had built amidst the undergrowth and in the trees, from where he could watch the wild animals. He showed us a platform of bamboo between two branches of a tree.

'That's where we're going tonight to wait for boars. If we're above ground level, they can't get our scent.'

Towards evening, it grew bitterly cold. Gerard, who had thought of everything, dug in his luggage and produced sweaters for Oeroeg and me in which we practically disappeared. Mist crept up out of all sides of the ravines and seemed to shut us off from the plain below. We were not accustomed to this cold that went to the very marrow of our bones, and we stood shivering, but Gerard kept us at our jobs and sent us into the woods with Ali for new supplies of wood. After darkness fell, we sat around the fire that Gerard had made in front of the cabin. We spoke Sundanese, only natural because of the presence of Oeroeg and Ali. On these occasions it appeared that the otherwise taciturn coolie, who made himself so inconspicuous that he nearly seemed a part of the scenery, was a born story-teller.

'Listen!' said Gerard enthusiastically, with the pride of an impresario. 'He knows dozens of stories!'

Ali did not need to be asked twice. He sat on his haunches closer to the fire and pulled the striped blanket around his shoulders. His gestures were so solemn that he appeared to be narrating for a ceremony. He spoke softly, and without the nuances in the volume of his voice and intonation which are generally considered to be inseparately associated with good story-telling. But I have never heard stories told in such a gripping manner as Ali's. His voice had the same quality of the stillness of the night all around us, the tone of the waterfalls in the forest, the wind in the tree-tops. Without the slightest effort on our part, we could imagine ourselves in that shadowy world of fables and myths of demigods and miraculous creatures. Oeroeg knew some of the tales, and could suddenly interrupt Ali by mentioning a name or fact before it was time for it to appear in the story. Ali did not like this. After such an interruption, he would be silent for a few moments and then spit into the fire. After an expectant silence during which I secretly nudged Oeroeg to indicate that he should keep his mouth shut, the narrator continued.

We went to sleep early, in so far as there could be any question of sleep on the hard boards of the bunks, each of which had room for four persons. With our blankets wrapped around us, we listened to the sounds of the night outside: the pelting of the water from the spout behind the cabin, and the rustling of the wind in the forest made us fall into a kind of half-sleep, which seemed to have lasted only a few seconds when Gerard woke us, usually between three and four o'clock. Oeroeg and I were ready in minutes, too excited to feel any fatigue. In the light of Gerard's pocket torch, our shadows, wild and ghostlike, danced along the walls of the cabin. Gerard instructed us to walk softly and to refrain from talking as soon as we were well into the forest. Then we set off, Gerard in front and Ali bringing up the rear of the procession. In the ominous darkness of the forest, Oeroeg and I at first forgot a great many of the plans we had made at home in anticipation of these expeditions: we would steal through the woods, unsheathed chopping-knives in our hands, fully prepared to attack panthers and wild boars. This *branie* (daredeviltry) of ours was gone now, but a trace of it returned as soon as we were sitting, high and dry, on the platform between the tree branches. The forest seemed filled with a ceaseless rustling, but Ali, who had the torch in his keeping, exhorted us to be patient. Now and then he would cast a beam of light into the darkness, and then we saw one or two, or even a whole herd of wild boars in the open spaces between the trees. The echoes of the shots resounded; and then, all around, there was a cracking, and a shuffling of animals fleeing rapidly through the bushes.

At that time, Gerard was—and for a long time afterwards continued to be—our leader, our vade-mecum, the infallible authority on every problem that confronted us. The other employees considered him eccentric, since he did not like drinking or playing bridge, or the weekly excursions to the *soos* (club) in Soekaboemi. He was one of those people who could take pleasure in complete solitude. We never found him idle when we went to see him in the evenings. He was fond of us, and regarded us as housemates from whom he had no secrets. We spoke by turns Dutch and Sundanese, however it happened to come out. Oeroeg understood Dutch, and could read it too, but a sort of shame constrained him from expressing himself in our language. When we urged him, he made a shy grimace, and mumbled a refusal. Not a word escaped him, however, of the conversations that Gerard and I held in Dutch.

I had less contact than ever with my father. He worked long hours in the factory and came home late in the afternoon. I usually saw him only at the dining-table. He ate quickly, often without saying a word. His thoughts were elsewhere, on his work, on matters that I had no conception of. I knew nothing about him, nor about what he was thinking or feeling. He had grown thinner, and his skin had become tanned. The bare spots on his temples and on the crown of his head were wider. From his nostrils to the corners of his mouth and chin ran two furrows that gave him a severe, but at the same time, pitiful appearance. I knew that the people on the plantation regarded him as a stickler for duty, an exaggeratedly precise person, who knew no clemency, neither for himself nor for his subordinates when it came to errors or neglect. The former fits of almost boyish jollity, of laughing and joking with employees or guests, belonged for good to the past. For that matter, we never had guests any more, and since the Bollinger affair, there seemed to be a void between my father and his employees. After the evening meal, he usually sat in the inner gallery, which, now stripped of everything that was not essential or useful, made the same impersonal impression as a hotel room. He smoked or read a detective story or a western in well-fingered and brightly coloured covers that the former administrator had left behind in the house for lonely evenings. Sometimes he put a record on the gramophone, and I felt then already, though only half-aware of it, that there could be nothing sadder in the world than marches and waltzes from operettas in the chill of a house that is not a home.

When Oeroeg and I were not with Gerard in his little house, we sat at the table on the back veranda with our maths and language books. Occasionally, my father would stand beside us looking over our shoulders. He picked up our copybooks and asked about our progress. Before signing the reports that we brought home every quarter, he studied them thoroughly, but as we never got bad marks, he had no reason to find fault. Oeroeg's handwriting was beautiful, in precise imitation of the examples given in school, the letters faultless in size and proportion. Seeing this, my father once asked Oeroeg if he had ever thought of his future.

'You could be an office clerk,' he said reflectively, as he looked through the copybook again. Oeroeg, smiling, cast his eyes sidewards, under half-closed eyelids, which he often did when he was at a loss for an answer.

'Oeroeg and I are going to be train engineers, or pilots,' I said hastily. 'But what we really want,' I added, 'is to be explorers.'

My father laid the copybook down on the table, and shrugged his shoulders. This was probably not the first time he realized that he could not speak to us as adults. Mixing easily with children was alien to my father. We lived alongside each other, with no contact, like beings who spoke different languages.

And yet I know that my father pondered the problem of my education. A few days before my eleventh birthday, he came to my bedroom just as I was about to go to bed. He watched me while I hung my clothes over a chair and brushed my teeth. It reminded me of the similar visit of my mother, years ago, when she came to tell me that I was going to school.

'Make a list of things you would like to have,' began my father. I nodded. I thought of asking for rifles for Oeroeg and me, that we could take along when we went hunting, but I strongly doubted whether my father would see the necessity of such a gift.

'In a few months I'm going on leave,' continued my father. 'I want to do some travelling, to see something of the world while I can still permit myself to do so. You understand that I cannot take you with me. I have thought of sending you to Holland, to a boarding-school maybe. At the end of this course, you'll be doing your matriculation exams, and you have to go to the HBS, the secondary school. And the life here ...,' he gesticulated. 'This way you're deprived. You're just like one of the natives, and that bothers me.'

Still standing at the sink, I braced myself.

'I don't want to go to Holland,' I burst out. Gerard's stories flashed through my mind: rain and cold, stuffy rooms, dull city streets. 'I want to stay here,' I repeated, 'and Oeroeg....'

My father interrupted me with an impatient gesture.

'Oeroeg, Oeroeg,' he said irritably. 'Always Oeroeg. Some day you'll have to live without Oeroeg. You've been friends with him too long for me. Don't you ever play with boys in your class? Ask some of them to come here for your birthday. We can pick them up and take them home in the car.'

'I know you're attached to Oeroeg,' he added, when he saw my face. 'It was inevitable. I had to do something for the boy. But as soon as Oeroeg finishes school, he'll go to work, and you have to continue your studies. Besides,' he hesitated a moment before continuing, 'you can certainly understand, son. You're European!'

I did think about this, but remained unimpressed by my father's last remark that I was European.

At my father's insistence, I invited two classmates to spend the Sunday after my birthday at the plantation. I had not been given the guns, but I did get a stamp album and a paint box, which I later gave, in secret, to Oeroeg. Gerard brought me the skin of a flying squirrel, fully treated, to hang on the wall. He also decorated the back gallery with Chinese lanterns and coloured paper streamers, which lent a festive note to the otherwise constrained birthday party. The two boys, strangers really, since at school I had only casual contact with them, chiefly in games to test our skill and in mutual braggadocio during the quarter-hour recess, took a look at my room and my possessions, and with my father and me partook of the *rijsttafel*, which was somewhat more elaborate for the occasion. Oeroeg had not been invited to this birthday dinner, and I was angry and disappointed, the more so since I had spoken to him about it, taking it for granted that he would be there. Oeroeg seemed unconcerned. While we were eating, I saw him watching us from the garden. After the meal, my father took me and my guests to the factory, where he gave us an instructive explanation of everything that was to be seen there. For the rest of the afternoon, we were sent into the garden to entertain ourselves. Oeroeg joined us. It was during these games that I became aware, for the first time in my life, that, in the eyes of others, Oeroeg was a 'native'—and not a native Indonesian like our classmate Harsono Hadiwijono, who was the son of a regent, but a village boy, the son of a subordinate employee of the plantation. The difference was in the slightly commanding tone my guests used, in the '*Ajo*—Come on, then!', the way they exhorted him to hurry up in the game we were playing. But what made me redden in annoyance hardly seemed to touch Oeroeg. Only once did I see him look sideways, as though he was turning his gaze inwards, his face and body assuming a scarcely perceptible rigidity, when one of my classmates, more out of mischief than evil intent, addressed to him an ugly Sundanese term of abuse.

After this incident, Oeroeg gradually withdrew, the rest of the afternoon contenting himself with sitting on the balustrade of the back veranda and watching us. That night, when I returned after taking my guests home, I could not find him anywhere. It was the first time that I did not know where he was or what he was doing. I went to see Gerard, who was smoking on the front porch of his house with his long legs on the table. I climbed up on a chair. For a time, neither of us said a word. Gerard possessed to a high degree the tact to wait in silence when he surmised that a confidence was impending. Finally, I came out with the problem that was tormenting me.

'Is Oeroeg less than us?' I burst out. 'Is he different?'

'Don't be a fool,' said Gerard calmly, without taking the pipe out of his mouth. 'Who said that?'

I told him, expressing myself with difficulty, about what I had perceived that afternoon.

'A panther is different from a monkey,' said Gerard, after a pause, 'but is the one inferior to the other? You think that's an idiotic question, don't you? You're right. And always find that idiotic when it concerns people. Being different is natural. Everybody is different from everybody else. I'm different from you. But being inferior or superior because of the colour of your face or because of your father's job—that's nonsense. Oeroeg is your friend, isn't he? If he can be your friend, how can he ever be *less* than you, or anybody else?'

When I walked back to the house in the dark, I heard Oeroeg's voice at the back, in the servants' quarters. The houseboy, the gardener, and Oeroeg were sitting beside each other on the low wall of the well and were discussing a cock that Danoeh had purchased the day before. I was about to go to them, but on second thoughts, decided not to. I fetched my new paint box from the back veranda and took it to the small room next to the kitchen where Oeroeg slept. A *klamboe* hung loosely from a piece of wire above the *bale-bale* (wooden couch). Oeroeg's copybooks and schoolbooks lay piled up neatly on top of an over-turned crate. On the whitewashed wall, he had pasted clippings of planes and racing cars. I knew that he was very proud of his bare, orderly room that was never entirely free of penetrating odours from the kitchen, and where, especially at night, a chilly dampness rose up from the cement floor. I put the paint box on the *bale-bale*, beside an old pair of my pyjamas that, like most of my worn clothes, had found their way, via the *baboe*, to Oeroeg.

Soekaboemi

My father decided that, in any case until matriculation exams, I should stay in the Indies. Since his substitute would come to live in the administrator's residence, efforts were made to find a place for me to live in Soekaboemi. I knew very little of all this. My father presented me with a *fait accompli* by taking me on a drive with him to

Soekaboemi, to the home of a person who for the rest of my life I shall call Lida. Lida was a woman of indeterminate age. At the time I am telling about now, I take her to have been between thirty and forty. She was one of those women who, from adulthood to ripe old age, never change outwardly. She was of medium height and rather thin; she had ash-blond hair that she wore short and straight, with bangs on her forehead, and grey eyes in an otherwise plain and irregular face. A few years ago, she had come to the Indies from Holland as a nurse, with the intention of setting up a rest-home in the cool mountain air of Soekaboemi. The friend and colleague who was to help her carry out her plan had rushed into marriage scarcely two months after her arrival in the tropics, leaving Lida poorer with regard to help as well as capital. The large hotels and *pensions* that were mushrooming all over Soekaboemi made it impossible for her to compete. What finally remained of the big project was only a small house with accommodation for a few persons. Lida could not be choosy: she accepted not only people who came for a rest, but vacationers, guests who stayed for only a few days, and even for meals. She had a reputation as being helpful and inexpensive: an agreeable, accommodating landlady.

The headmaster of my school, who knew Lida, had recommended her as a temporary housemother and caregiver for me while my father was on leave. Lida's house had absolutely nothing of the Indies about it. It might have been on the Veluwe, in typically Dutch towns like Laren or Blaricum. It had climbing plants over the façade and the roof, a built-on sun parlour, and a garden full of roses. Cushions, centre-pieces, tea cosies, and handmade carpets adorned the interior, which seemed to have been furnished with a burning fireplace in mind. I gazed in amazement at the wainscoted walls, the cluttered rooms, the drapes and window curtains. Lida, who was prepared for our visit, served us tea and came to the point at once. I had the impression that my father had already made her acquaintance and that my future stay at her house was indeed an accomplished fact. I was told that I would soon be moving. The resolute way in which Lida spoke and the suddenness of the whole matter took me so by surprise that in the beginning I had no chance, nor desire, to let my voice be heard.

'But ... Oeroeg?' I finally blurted out, when there was a lull in the conversation. 'What's going to happen to Oeroeg if I have to stay here?'

Lida looked at me with her friendly, somewhat myopic eyes.

'Who is Oeroeg?' she asked, and when my father began impatiently to reply, she continued quickly, 'No, *you* tell me,' and to my father, 'let him tell me himself.'

I struggled over my words. I'm afraid that what I said was confused; but how could I explain in only a few words who and what Oeroeg was? Oeroeg was my friend, practically since my birth the only living being around me with whom I had shared every phase of my existence, every thought, every experience. And not only that. Oeroeg was more than that. Oeroeg represented—although I could not express it—my life on and around Kebon Djati: climbing through the woods and mountains; playing in the garden and on the stones in the river; riding in the train, going to school: the alphabet of my childhood.

My father explained to me briefly that Oeroeg would stay on the plantation.

'He can walk back and forth to the station—it's not that

far,' he decided. 'And otherwise, we'll find a way out. It's nothing for you to worry about.'

I began, not wrongly, to suspect that my father considered my living at Lida's a means to break off my attachment to Oeroeg. I was full of bitterness at the injustice of this, and during the last weeks of my stay at the plantation I had stayed as far away as possible from my father. I played truant often, over a long period of time, and the headmaster complained; it was this that gave Lida the idea to let Oeroeg, who was a party to the offence, come to her house. Oeroeg and I were then in our twelfth year, an age when any thwarting of inclinations leads to stubborn and often secret resistance.

We stayed away from school, in the beginning just to wander around the town talking about the happenings in this new life of ours, but later, when we were already accustomed to the changed situation, to act like hooligans, only the two of us, or together with a group of half-grown native Indonesian boys, in the markets and the shopping district. Oeroeg, who, as I later realized, was then much more mature than I, seemed hardly, or not at all shocked at the way our cronies in these street adventures initiated us into aspects of life that we had never before encountered. One of them, Jules, an Indo of about fifteen, with a face disfigured by smallpox, was the son of a prostitute who was visited by employees of nearby plantations. She lived in a small annexe in a sordid, noisy lane, more like an alley, on the periphery of the kampong. Once he enticed us to come to his house to eat *ketan*, a delicacy made from rice, grated coconut, and brown sugar. His mother, who let us call her Sonya, was sitting on her porch steps, barefoot and wearing a dirty pink kimono. The small yard was full of garbage and pieces of broken bottles. Jules, without embarrassment, walked ahead of us through the untidy bedroom full of cheap baubles and paper flowers. In his conversation, he was not sparing of particulars that had to do with the life his mother led. I tried, imitating Oeroeg, not to show any confusion, but only partly succeeded. In some way or other, I had to react to these new experiences, and this I did by being unmanageable at school and whimsically moody at Lida's.

Another unsavoury character, even more so than Jules, was Adi, a nimble native Indonesian boy who carried out petty thievery in the shops of the city with the self-assurance of a professional. It was through him too that for the first time in our lives we found ourselves in a movie-house—a structure full of wooden benches where only old, silent cowboy and gangster films were shown. These expressly linked series of robbery, murder, and mayhem had an enormous influence on us. We were so fascinated by the movies that we were willing to try any means to obtain the enjoyment they provided.

It was just at this time that Lida, even though unaware of the actual state of things, intervened. Lida had what Oeroeg and I in later years would call a 'soft soap mentality'—no imagination, no understanding of or even belief in the existence of things that she had no conception of, an ineradicable lack of suspicion of which she was again and again the dupe. She was bourgeois without being narrow and she strove to be good in the Christian sense without being a bigot. She measured everyone and everything according to the standard of her own immaculate, absolutely unimaginative, practical spirit. All these qualities were attractive because of the fact that she had no

prejudices and was utterly honest. Obviously, she was un-
lucky in her association with the native Indonesians, especially servants and tradespeople. Her sense of loyalty, her
tendency to resolve conflicts and misunderstandings by
means of logical and patient argument, caused astonishment
and distrust. A display of authority to maintain prestige
was completely foreign to her. Even people of goodwill
stole from her and deceived her, only as a result of a lack of
mutual understanding. The many servants who came and
went were all aware of this, but Lida was not.

From the very beginning, Lida was fond of Oeroeg.
Perhaps his loneliness stimulated her maternal instinct, or
he satisfied the obsession she had, albeit subconsciously,
for the exotic, which had certainly been the reason for her
journey to the Indies in the first place, and which had
not been fulfilled in her new work and situation. It is also
possible that the beginning of Oeroeg's development, from
village boy to scholar, reminded her of her own difficult
youth, of the manner in which she had had to escape from
a narrow, uneducated milieu.

Oeroeg had a harmoniously slender, muscled physique,
in contrast to my ungainly, as yet undeveloped limbs. It
looked as though I would grow tall, which proved later to
be the case. Oeroeg's slight build, his large eyes whose
pupils were like mirrors of ink floating in the bluish whites
of the eyes and which were sharply outlined like the eyes
of a *wayang* (shadow play) puppet, his wide but well-formed
mouth, and his entire attitude, a combination of ironic reserve and shyness, enchanted Lida. Oeroeg's visits turned
into overnight stays, and after a few months, he moved to
the *pension* for good. Indeed there were reasons to be
found to justify this step. Our personnel at Kebon Djati

were now strictly disciplined by the wife of the substitute administrator; she regarded Oeroeg as no more than a relative staying with the houseboy, and she had taken away his room next to the kitchen. He now slept with Danoeh behind the old stables. The clothes he wore, cast-offs of mine, were dingy and uncared for, his hair had not been cut for a long time. He made a neglected impression.

'If your father pays for the boy's schooling, someone has to take care of him,' Lida said in explanation of her decision to take Oeroeg into her house. An extra bed was shoved into my bedroom and an extra chair pulled up at the table. The few guests Lida had at the time ate in their own rooms. In this way, Oeroeg again made his entrance into my immediate surroundings, this time indisputably as a playmate and housemate.

I knew that Lida corresponded with my father, and I assumed that Oeroeg's moving in with us, as well as his future, was discussed in her letters. Now and then, bits of news trickled down to us. Lida's enquiries at the Dutch–Native School revealed that Oeroeg was among the most gifted of the pupils. He was quick-witted, and demonstrated a dedication to his studies that was not diminished by occasional bouts of restlessness. The headmaster knew of my father's plan to employ Oeroeg on the plantation as a clerk after the seven years of primary school; he was of the opinion, however, that better things were reserved for a boy of Oeroeg's abilities, and he advised that the boy should continue his education at the secondary school.

Lida was elated at this discovery and wrote about it in great detail; but my father had no sympathy with the idea. He foresaw considerable costs with relatively few results, since in the end the professional possibilities for Oeroeg were restricted. During the afternoons and evenings, Lida sat with us doing her mending while we were busy with our homework. An idea had taken root in her brain that she could not shake off. I can still see her sitting there, forever pushing back the spectacles that she had to wear when she was sewing. Oeroeg and I, who were otherwise quite fond of her, would smile meaningfully at each other about the nonchalant way she sat back in the low cane chair so that the pink elastic bands around her thighs were visible. She usually wore shapeless dresses with puffed sleeves, of cheap flowered material that was sold in the markets in unlimited quantities. Little did we suspect what was going on her mind while she sewed buttons on our shirts and mended our trousers, how, in those quiet hours, a plan was ripening, the execution of which was to compensate her for her failed nursing home scheme. Oeroeg had to get ahead; Oeroeg had to be given the opportunity to develop himself. From the moment she had put this into her head, she went to work systematically.

Since Lida's knowledge of Malay and Sundanese was poor, we always spoke Dutch in her presence. Oeroeg had somewhat overcome his previous shyness, although he still preferred to listen in silence. Now Lida began energetically to take him in hand; his pronunciation must be improved. Not a day passed without her speaking at great length about the importance of the medical profession, about the great need in the tropics for medical personnel for the sake of the people. She stated facts and figures on epidemics and brought home books and brochures for us, especially Oeroeg, to read. She raked up all the material from the time of her own studies, showing us illustrations of internal organs and their structure, the position of the blood vessels and muscles. In the beginning, we looked at all the pictures more out of politeness than great interest. I was surprised that when Lida finally decided to put the question to Oeroeg directly as to whether he wanted to be a doctor, he answered, 'Maybe,' followed almost immediately by 'Yes.' That evening, in our room, I reproached him for renouncing our ideal of becoming pilots.

'Ah, what of it?' said Oeroeg, with his own distinctive accent, 'if that's what she wants.'

'What do you think of Lida?' I asked. It was the first time I had brought myself to think about putting into words the feelings we had with respect to this woman who took care of us. Oeroeg glanced at me with his dark, side-long look before he answered.

'Not bad,' he said finally. He then made a derisive grimace and gave a realistic imitation of the way Lida ne-gotiated with a *klontong*, a Chinese vendor, which made us roll over on our beds in hilarious laughter until the guests in the adjoining room knocked on the wall and Lida came rushing in to us to calm us down.

My matriculation exams came at about the same time as my father's return. I had not seen him in well over a year. He was much heavier, and sun-tanned, and this, with his well-fitting palm beach suit, gave him for the first time the appearance of the traditional planter. I was amazed at his boisterous high spirits, and the generosity with which he distributed gifts—but even more so at the fact that he had brought along a new wife, something he had not men-tioned in any of his letters. They had been married in Singapore, and she was still in Batavia to do some shop-ping. Lida refrained from making any comments, but it was obvious that she was very critical of the way my father did things. Oeroeg, without any form of process, went from one guardian to another, and it was decided that I would spend the long holiday on the plantation. My father no longer talked about sending me to Holland, presumably in connection with the expense. At least, this appeared to me as a possibility when I made the acquaintance of my stepmother, who hated unnecessary expenditures. She was a fresh, practical, businesslike young woman, with a pretty, but expressionless face. From the very beginning, I disliked her because of the inflexible manner in which she organized Kebon Djati, because of her high-handed authoritarian conduct towards the employees. As a governess and schoolteacher she had spent a few years in relative subordination, and it seemed she had decided to compensate for what she had suffered now that she was the wife of an administrator.

At home she was indisputably the boss. My father greatly admired her efficiency and was visibly charmed by her health and energy. In contrast to my mother, who had always risen late and seldom changed from her negligée into morning clothes, Eugenie sat at the breakfast table with my father neatly dressed and with the household activities in full swing. As often as possible, I escaped from this new atmosphere. Usually I went to see Oeroeg in Soekaboemi, or somewhere outside the town, going on outings in the neighbourhood or swimming in one of the mountain pools. Lida had taken over a *pension* in Batavia, and Oeroeg and I would go there in September. Oeroeg was going to the junior high school, and after that he would go to the Dutch East Indies Medical College in Soerabaya. Lida had mapped out the whole course of action.

We paid a visit to Sidris, who hardly knew what to say to her son. She looked at him with amazement and pride on her face, and shook her head, almost powerless to understand the situation. In the course of the years, her house had lost every trace of Western comfort. A few soiled mats served as chairs on the primitive front porch, garbage lay in piles in the yard, and it stank everywhere of dried salted fish and fish paste. Satih, now definitely too heavy, and wearing a sarong and tight camisole, sat in the doorway plaiting her shining strands of hair into a knot. She told us that she did not want to stay in the village; she wanted to go to the city and work as a *baboe*. Oeroeg and I squatted among Sidris and the children, for the first time in our lives not feeling at home there. The one year of order and regularity in Lida's spotless house had made us feel an unsuspected inner constraint with regard to the squalor and poverty of the village. Among his raggedly dressed brothers and sisters, Oeroeg was a prince. We ate together with the family: rice and a sort of crisp dry biscuit of dried ground shrimp. Oeroeg took leave of his family, and we started back.

It was the hottest time of day, and we sauntered down the road strewn with rough stones. Huge, foamy clouds, flattened underneath as though they were floating on glass, travelled by in the bright noonday sky. The green on the mountain slopes glistened in the light. All around reigned the languorous silence that makes the land seem deserted during the hottest hours. Only the distant barking of a dog and the monotonous tinkling of the bells of water-buffaloes reached us over the fields. No living soul was in sight on the road or on the rice paddies, nor were there any coloured head-cloths of the tea-pickers to be seen among the green tea plants higher up on the mountain. On the bushes along the verge of the road glittered hundreds of *tambleang* flowers, in all shades of pink, red, and orange, under a swarm of butterflies.

Oeroeg suggested a swim in the river, which, half-concealed under clusters of shrubs, streamed over the stones with an inviting plash. We threw our clothes into a heap among the greenery, and entered the fresh, crystal-clear water. It was impossible to really swim in the bowl-shaped pools between the stones, and we threw ourselves into the water stretching out full length or leaning back against the bubbling water falling on rocks ranged together like stairs. We had refreshed ourselves in the river like this hundreds of times during the years we had spent at Kebon Djati. Surrendering completely to the seething, splashing water, leaping among the rocks, revelling in the countless games we played in the river—these were among the most intense experiences of our childhood. This time, however, in a kind of disappointed surprise, Oeroeg and I realized that we were not wholeheartedly enjoying ourselves. Perhaps that is putting it too strongly. It might be better to say that at that moment—and from that time on—swimming meant no more to us than a refreshing plunge, an action taken from an all-absorbing need to be cooled off; and as long as this desire was satisfied, there was no longer any reason for either of us to stay in the water. Even though we were well aware of this, we continued splashing around, out of habit, and probably too, out of a sort of mutual feeling of embarrassment. The difference was that we saw the swimming, the river, the sparkling water, with other eyes, with eyes that could no longer see the real world as a world of wonders. Gone was the magical kingdom in which we had been heroes and explorers. The shadowy caves were no more than shady spots under the low-hanging foliage on the banks; the hunting ground of rocky plateaus and unbridgeable rapids was only a mountain stream, rippling through its bed of gravel and larger stones. Crabs and dragon-flies shot by in unchanging alluring nuances of colour under and above the surface, but they no longer stimulated our imagination, although we chased them out of a kind of sportiveness. As we lay stretched out on a flat stone, the real significance of these changes flashed through me. I looked at Oeroeg, and in his eyes saw the same discovery. Something had passed away. Our childhood was gone.

Batavia

Eugenie was expecting a child. I had no trouble persuading my father to allow me to go to the secondary school in Batavia. On the contrary, I had the impression that for him this was an unexpected solution to a pressing problem. There was no question, however, of my staying at Lida's—I was to be quartered in a boarding establishment connected with the school. I left for Batavia shortly before the school year began. Oeroeg and Lida had left a few weeks earlier. I was not familiar with the city, and in the beginning was quite impressed by the large squares, the white buildings, and the busy traffic. The boarding house was an old East Indies house with dark rooms and tiled floors. It lay deep among other palatial residences, on a piece of ground that at least on the street side, consisted of a scorched stretch of grass. A few enormous succulent plants with thorny leathery leaves stood like sentries on either side of the entrance. The school was run by a married couple, both teachers; the husband supervised the boys' schoolwork and the wife managed the household. A look at the interior revealed that the first consideration was order and practicality, with nowhere an excess of furniture or decoration. The white-walled, bare-floored bedrooms accommodated four students, with four of everything: four beds, four small cupboards, four chairs, four clothes-racks. The beds with their stiffly hanging *klamboe*, cubes of mosquito-netting, here, more than anywhere else, resembled cages. The windows were barred with a view to the possibility of burglars. I shared the room with three older boys, who hardly took any notice of me, except for borrowing my pencils and tearing pages out of my copybooks which they then used as scrap paper.

The daily schedule was very simple. After breakfast, at seven o'clock, we went to school, via the back garden that bordered on the schoolyard. We returned at one o'clock, when we had a meal on the back veranda. We sat at three or four long tables, and without much talk, which was actually more or less forbidden, worked our food inside. From two to three, it was rest hour, which usually meant absolute quiet. We read, napped, or did homework, the latter with the idea of being exempted, in the evening, from working under supervision, which all of us hated. We usually did our homework in the inner veranda, where old desks and tables stood suggestively in rows. After tea we went there to labour over compositions and maths problems until dinnertime. Those whose homework had been checked according to their schedules were free until

eight o'clock. Clearly, no full and positive growth and development could be expected in such a barren atmosphere.
Occasionally, pent-up feelings managed to vent themselves
in bursts of hooliganism and forced smutty talk. In general,
there was no real friendship among the boys. During every
semester, there were more or less permanent alliances, but
that was all. With the exception of a few of my housemates,
I did not feel attracted to them. I took part in the pranks
and the secret dirty talk, but for the rest the whole business
left me cold.

Often, when I had done my homework, and in any case
most of every Sunday, I went to see Oeroeg and Lida. The
pension that Lida had taken over was in a run-down neighbourhood, which had considerably declined in 'standing'
during the past ten years. The houses, occupied by Chinese
and Indo families, made a neglected impression. Small native shops and *warung* rose up among the larger residences,
and in that way seemed to push the kampong that bordered
on the gardens towards the street. Lida, who had no eye
for these things, had put a rope around her neck by this
exchange of *pensions*. Even though her garden was reason-
ably well cared for and her front veranda freshly painted,
the surroundings worked against her. Even the proud sign
by the gate, 'Pension Huize Oud-Bussum' was no advert-
isement in this atmosphere. She had a handful of guests: a
few bachelors who worked in downtown offices and were
seldom home except for the evening meal; an elderly couple
who had known better days in 'sugar', but since the depres-
sion lived in poverty they could no longer deny; and two
young women who, not to Lida, but so much the more to
Oeroeg and me, appeared to be of doubtful morals. Assisted
by an insolent houseboy and three slovenly *baboe*, Lida

served her boarders, who occupied similarly furnished rooms, provided with a front veranda and a set of chairs.

The heat and the fuss and bother of her life in Batavia did not agree with Lida. She was not as fresh and cheerful as she had been in Soekaboemi, and she had practically no time for us. She was usually to be found sitting in her office, a stuffy den in one of the outbuildings, with a pile of bills in front of her. Her bangs stuck to her damp forehead and her flowered dress was soiled at the neck. When I came to see Oeroeg in the afternoons, she greeted me absent-mindedly and sent us to the kitchen to ask for lemonade or tea.

For Oeroeg, Lida spared neither expense nor trouble. He looked immaculate in a white polo shirt and linen shoes. He no longer wore his *pici*. When I asked him about this, he made an impatient gesture and a clacking noise with his tongue. 'I'm not a Muslim,' he explained later; and indeed I had never seen him show much interest in his religion, although at Kebon Djati he had gone to the mosque with our houseboy. By not wearing the *pici*, however, he had lost something. His European clothes, his thick, fashionably cut hair, took away from him to a certain extent the modesty, the typical native reserve, that to me had always been such a part of him. He was happy at school, he told me: his junior high school was attended by boys and girls of all ethnic groups; and he had no trouble at all with his schoolwork. I noticed, not without annoyance, that he had taken over the mannerisms and speech of the Indo boys. Troops of them would burn up the roads of the city on multicoloured racing bikes, flamboyantly dressed in imitation of film and sports heroes. Oeroeg smoked now, which Lida merely winked at, tolerant of anything he did. She was proud of her foster child and did everything possible for him. She and Oeroeg both had bedrooms in the outbuildings, but Oeroeg's was larger and better furnished than hers.

Lida's greatest grievance was the attitude of her *pension* guests with respect to her and Oeroeg—even she herself had noticed it: a critical attitude, full of ridicule. She was too unsuspecting to understand the deeper meaning of their gossiping. Oeroeg felt it, but seemed to be somewhat amused at it. He had nothing to do with the two single men; with respect to the old couple, he was downright arrogant; and as to the two young women, I had never seen him so insolent as in their presence. When we wandered through the garden in the afternoons, they sat on their small front veranda, busy polishing their nails or engaged in some other cosmetic activity. In floppy kimonos, un- kempt hair, and with worn slippers on their feet, they rocked back and forth in their cane chairs, leaning back with their legs on the railing in their free and easy manner. They called out to us, making facetious remarks, and it was usually not until later that I became aware of the *double entendre* of what they were saying. Oeroeg smiled his secret smile, and out of the corner of his eye gazed at something else, as though embarrassed. And yet we always trifled with the girls. They would bring out jars of candied tamarind or *goelali*, and Oeroeg and I always ended up sitting on the porch railing eating their sweets while the banter became increasingly naughtier. Half-smiling, Oeroeg could say the coarsest things, directing his eyes straight at the girls, and this inscrutable gaze of his confused them so that they did not know whether to be angry or not. Usually, they hit him or kicked him playfully, and tried to start a romp.

Although I felt that I really ought to find the behaviour of these girls distasteful, I was none the less fascinated by their talk and their teasing. I always felt guilty when Lida called to tell me that it was time to go back to the dormitory.

I was amazed at how calm Oeroeg was when he walked a short way back with me and after some abusive words about the two girls, lit a cigarette. It seemed then that I had much less contact with him than before. The problems of adolescence I was struggling with seemed not to exist for him. Compared with him, I felt green and foolish. Perhaps the way my freedom of movement was restricted was one reason I felt inferior. Oeroeg could do whatever he wanted in the evenings, while I, except on rare occasions, was very seldom given permission to go into town.

I do not know what feelings Lida had that made her so devoted to Oeroeg. I can only make assumptions. I merely describe the events as they presented themselves at the time. I can never again ask the persons concerned to explain what they said and did. As regards Lida's motives, I am still in the dark. Sometimes I think it was her own loneliness that drove her to take care of Oeroeg, an inner need to find, among all her fellows, one person to whom she could give help and guidance. After all, for women who choose the nursing profession, being a nurse is an escape valve for the deepest unfulfilled instincts. Sometimes it seemed to me that it was Oeroeg who brought her—and me, and other people he associated with—under his spell; that he possessed one of those strange passive personalities that exert an irresistible attraction on their surroundings.

During Oeroeg's years at the junior high school, he lost entirely the characteristics that in Soekaboemi had stamped him as a village boy. On the contrary, I had the impression that he was doing his utmost to undo everything that would remind him of the past. He spoke only Dutch now, and he wore conspicuously Western clothes. He was never on familiar terms with Lida's personnel. He preferred to ignore any allusions to our childhood, to Sidris, and to his brothers and sisters. The only time he was ever on the point of flying out at me was when I once talked about his father in the presence of some of his school friends. I was overcome with surprise when I discovered that Oeroeg was doing his best to pass himself off as an Indo. I knew that he had always had a feeling of dislike towards Indos that bordered on repugnance. But his desire to become assimilated into the world of the Europeans was so great that he was even capable of making this concession. The transition from the one walk of life to the other was made easier for him because he lived at Lida's and because he was continuously in contact with schoolmates 75 per cent of whom were of mixed blood and belonged to a group that just as persistently strove to imitate Western ways. I was once present when Oeroeg and Lida were discussing the possibility of Oeroeg using Lida's last name. I even remember Lida trying for a time to call Oeroeg Ed or Ted, or some similar name, but it was impossible to keep this up.

Occasionally, we went to the movies, which Oeroeg often visited alone. Cowboy films now interested us less than Tarzan and horror films, and we would also break the rules on the age limit for the sake of erotic sensations. After these visits to movie theatres, where we usually met some of Oeroeg's friends, we went to a Chinese café that rivalled an American drugstore in its service as well as its interior. Between nickle and glass, we sat on bar stools eating ices and *bami* (noodles), while an electric gramophone broadcast deafening jazz music through the shop. It was at this time too that we met girls, mostly sisters of Oeroeg's friends, dark, early-ripe types who put me in a state of bewilderment with their subtle giggling and endearments.

Oeroeg's choice among the girls was Poppie, with her light skin and fair hair. We learned to dance at Poppie's house; not being able to dance was then felt as a deficiency in our education. Poppie lived with her mother, very fat, and very Indo-Dutch, a divorced woman, in a new neighbourhood on the outskirts of the city. The small modern house was situated on a piece of land bleached in the fierce heat of the sun, where nothing seemed to want to grow. In the living-room, decorated with leaded windows, it was unbearably hot. With our clothes sticking to our bodies, we led the girls around in tangos or waltzes, to the accompaniment of the cheerless music of cracked gramophone records. Poppie's mother spread herself out over a chair, with a paper fan in her hand.

In those days, our recreation consisted mainly of dancing and going to the movies, but now and then we took trips on Sundays, usually to the harbour or to the tidal forests outside Priok. We wandered over the malodorous fish market, along the canal where prahus rigged with reddish-brown sails were sailing in. We walked as far as the lighthouse at the end of the narrow pier, where the disintegrating cement was overgrown with algae and slithery shells. Even the sea breeze brought no relief from the heat. The light, glowing white, vibrated over the harbour sheds of corrugated zinc above the docks sprinkled with coal-dust and the white houses surrounding the fish market. A vapour drifted over the sea, obstructing the view. Sometimes we swam away from the pier, chiefly to demonstrate how daring we were, since we knew that there were sharks in these waters. We were still more attracted by the tidal forests, in spite of the malarial mosquitoes that buzzed among the small sickly white branches. The earth where we could still walk was soft under our feet, and there hovered a briny odour of decay. Where plants and trees thrust their way out of the water, there was a continuous sucking sound around the roots, and on the surface of the layers of mud that formed the crossing between land and sea, air bubbles burst open. Here and there, we found a stretch of beach between the trees, but the water there would not tempt anyone to swim in it. Apart from that, the mosquitoes continued to bother us, lighting on us as soon as we took off our clothes. We usually walked some distance along the coast, one behind the other on the narrow path, stooping to avoid the tough stiltlike roots that blocked our passage. Wherever the ground was dry enough, we sat down.

Our conversations always revolved around the same topics: our schools, our mutual acquaintances, sports, movies, and girls. Once the question of our future came up. We were lying on the ground, knees pulled up, our handkerchiefs under our heads. All around us were swarms of insects that we tried to drive away with cigarette smoke. I told Oeroeg that I was planning to study engineering.

'And you?' I asked, after I had explained my motives in great detail. 'Are you still planning to go to the medical school? Is that what you really want to do?'

Oeroeg flung his cigarette stub far away into the bushes.

'Ah, why not?' was his indifferent reply. 'Anything. But an office is nothing for me. At least a doctor is his own boss.

They'll all come to me to be *cut*.' He illustrated his words with a series of sounds to imitate the cutting of someone's throat.

'Very nice for your patients,' I said. 'They'll be frightened to death of you!'

'All of them from the *desa*,' muttered Oeroeg, lighting a new cigarette. 'The *dukun* (shaman or native healer) kills many more of them, with his traditional herbs and his black magic. They prefer that to going to a real doctor.'

'That's true; but maybe they'll have more confidence in you because you're . . . ,' I began. I wanted to say 'because you're one of them,' but I swallowed the words when I saw Oeroeg's swift sidelong glance, dark and threatening, now that I'd dared to mention the forbidden subject.

'What are you going to do then—will you work for the government?' I asked hastily. I remembered having heard that there were scholarships available in the Indies for medical training.

Oeroeg shrugged. He was sitting on his heels, and the ease with which he balanced his whole body on the balls of his feet, as well as the relaxed line of shoulder, back, and hips, belied his origin.

'Maybe,' was his non-committal reply. After a brief silence, he added, 'Later, I want to go away from here.'

I sat up. 'To Holland?' I asked in surprise.

Oeroeg made the two-toned sound in his throat that in the Indies means yes. 'I'd rather go to America,' he said suddenly.

He had collected small pieces of rock and damaged shells and he threw them quickly one after the other at the dead branch of a tree not far from us. To Oeroeg, America was the land of promise: a country where we both imagined everything was bigger, better, and more beautiful than anywhere else in the world. Under the influence of the films we saw and the things we read, we imagined it as a place where skyscrapers and technical miracles were immediately bounded by the other extreme: the plains of the Wild West. But Oeroeg's desire was not only for adventure. I realized later that he believed—wrongly, after all—that in the New World, race and one's station in life, would be, neither for himself nor for others, of any consideration.

We talked about Lida. Oeroeg's relationship to her had never been clear to me. Looking back at the time I am writing about now, I cannot say that he treated her with love or even any notable respect. He seemed to regard as perfectly natural her good care of him, the sacrifices she was willing to make for him, her unflagging interest in his progress, her indulgence towards him, and her trust in him. As I have said before, Oeroeg was passive. He accepted the course his life had taken as he had previously accepted his life on Kebon Djati and his companionship with me. I doubt that there was any real contact between him and Lida. Oeroeg was quite tractable, and in general did what she wanted him to do without contradiction. Probably it was not even Lida's wish that there should be an emotional bond between them. She wanted only to have a part, as a beneficiary, in the development of this life that in all its forms of expression remained strange to her, but perhaps for that very reason, was so appealing. She herself was too modest, too sober as well, to show, or to desire, any feelings of affection. I can imagine that she considered herself rewarded by the good reports Oeroeg brought home, by his evolution from shabby native boy to intelligent student.

For that matter, she was too busy with her new work to pay much attention to him.

It was not smooth sailing for Lida in her 'Huize Oud-Bussum'. I am overcome by a strong feeling of pity when I think of how she plodded along in an environment that was hostile to her nature and ability. When Oeroeg was fifteen—he was then in the second year of junior high school—she discovered by accident that the afternoon visits he made to the young women in her *pension*, supposedly to get sweets or to run small errands for them, were not entirely of an innocent nature. I heard from Oeroeg later how it had all come about. There is no need to go into detail. For Lida, this was a blow in the face. She realized for the first time that this was an area in which Oeroeg needed guidance. It was characteristic of her that she did not believe Oeroeg was to blame. She gave the girls notice to leave, deaf to protests and obvious insinuations. She only reproached herself for allowing such a situation to occur in her house, even though she had no knowledge of it. But she was at a loss with respect to this new aspect of Oeroeg's education. She checked on him more carefully, and saw danger where there was none. The walks through the city with girls, the dancing lessons at Poppie's house, the frequenting of the movies—all this frightened her. She knew Oeroeg well enough to know that it was not the biological facts that she must impart to him, but the '*savoir vivre*' which would enable him to distinguish between refined and coarse, between style and stylelessness; the inner discipline; the proper reserve with respect to kitsch. Lida felt that it was a man's job to initiate a boy into these matters. She suddenly foresaw unsuspected conflicts if Oeroeg should spend the difficult years he still

had ahead of him in her *pension*; not that she feared a repe-
tition of the incidents with the girls, but because she was
not capable of enforcing the discipline the boy needed.
The obvious thing for her to do was to turn to the only
authority she knew of in her neighbourhood: the director
of my boarding-school. I do not know how Lida succeeded
in moving him to accept a boy who was so different from the
others in background and education. I have the feeling that
financial considerations played a greater role than idealistic
ones, but who can say? It is also possible that he liked Lida.

Oeroeg stayed at the boarding-school until the end of
his junior high school years. At first, he felt insulted and
hurt that he was now put under restraint. He hated our
strict daily schedule and the whole atmosphere of the
place. He was insolent and recalcitrant, violated the regulations on going out, and isolated himself, from me as well.
It gradually dawned on me that this attitude was not only
the result of an urge to be free or to resist authority, but for
a great part was the consequence of Oeroeg's desire to
make an impression on the other boys, since he knew that
he could only win their sympathy by such a demonstration
of *branie*. It was generally known that Oeroeg and I were
friends, and had been before he came to the boarding-
school. I had never made a secret of his origins, and I
found the opinions of the boys, in case they contained
criticism or ridicule, too unimportant for them to bother
me. Remarks like 'We saw you at Pasar Baru with your
djongos' or 'Have you been out with your native friend?'
had little effect on me, since they went no further than jest
and made my relationship with the boys at the school neither better nor worse. But this changed when Oeroeg
came. We soon came to live in a sort of isolation from the

others. I do not wish to imply that there was anything in this remotely resembling a boycott or demonstration—I'm sure that most of the boys were not even aware of anything. I do not know to what degree Oeroeg's own defiant attitude contributed to it. Daredevils were sooner honoured than avoided. What caused the distance was that Oeroeg was indefinably 'different'—it was the subtle difference in his behaviour and his nature, in his 'aura', I would say if I could put it into words.

There was no question of any hostility towards Oeroeg. It was more a sort of indifference, a lack of interest. His efforts in some way or another to make himself noticed led to nothing. I think Oeroeg was soon enough aware of all this. For a while, he persisted in being insolent and nonchalant, but then suddenly he fell into a state of withdrawal that I had never seen in him at Kebon Djati. He was extremely taciturn, and the dark, clouded look never left his eyes. We slept in the same room, but the presence of two other room-mates made any confidential conversations impossible. Besides, I doubt whether Oeroeg would have laid himself open. When we took walks, now very seldom, he kept carefully at a distance. It was not for nothing that I had lived close to Oeroeg for so long. In spite of the fact that I was occupied by the problems of my own adolescence— I had just as little guidance at the time—I felt, not without sympathy, where the shoe was pinching Oeroeg. In junior high school, he had had no difficulty maintaining a sense of equality, but with us it was different. Neither the way he dressed nor the way he acted could make him into what he seemed to want to be: one of us.

It was probably at this time that the estrangement between us began. Oeroeg could not do otherwise than identify me with the European group whose rejection he felt. I knew that he had stopped going around after school hours with his Indo friends. He was now often with a certain Abdullah Haroedin, a boy of half-Arab descent, who, like him, planned to go to the medical school. I was rather jealous of the friendship, which shut me out. I do not know whether this came about because of Oeroeg himself, or because of Abdullah. The fact was that we were seldom or never a threesome. Looking back, it seems to me that Oeroeg, by being with Abdullah, was looking for a counterbalance for the situation he found at the school. Abdullah was small and fat, with an intelligent face and curly hair. He wore glasses with large black frames, which made him look a bit comic. His sense of humour was closely related to Oeroeg's; they shared a world of thought from which, as I grew older, I became further and further removed. It often happened now that I no longer went to Lida's on Sundays or free evenings, because Oeroeg had already made an appointment with Abdullah. It bothered me, and once I made a comment about it. Oeroeg looked at me in silence, and it seemed to me even with a certain satisfaction. Any explanation or expression from either side was impossible.

During the holidays I sometimes went to Kebon Djati, which I found so absolutely different that it seemed to have been changed by magic. The house was full of new furniture, the garden was neatly laid out, with gravel paths and beautiful well-kept flower-beds. The servants all had new faces—I did not recognize any of them. Eugenie, who had gained weight and looked downright aggressive, wielded the sceptre, not only in the administrator's house, but probably over the entire plantation. My father appeared to be healthy and content. He had acquired a double chin, which hung over his collar, and, oddly enough, made him resemble one of the big frogs Oeroeg and I used to catch when we were children. When I saw him lying full-length in his chair, in a shirt with rolled-up sleeves and the belt of his trousers stretched over his pouch, I could hardly imagine that this was the same man who a few years ago had sat disconsolately next to a croaking gramophone. The gramophone was gone and in its place was my stepbrother's playpen. My father gave me a few letters my mother had written to me from Nice, where she now evidently made her home. The lavender, lightly perfumed stationery was distasteful to me. My mother wrote as though I was still a little boy and had enclosed a newspaper picture of a new racing car model. I saw Eugenie looking at it, and the blood rushed to my head. My mother also sent her regards to Oeroeg. 'What has happened to him?' I put the letters away in the cupboard of the guest-room, and decided not to answer them. Gerard was on leave, so my loneliness at Kebon Djati was complete.

I wandered through the tea gardens, the only place that had not changed, and that was as enchanting as ever. The bitter fragrance of the green leaves, the flowers of the flame trees against the sky, the voices of the tea-pickers audible far away in the silence—it was all still the same, and here the passing of the years seemed unimportant and as fleeting as a dream. I sat in the grass on the edge of a ravine and gazed over the expanse of land that was covered with a bluish mist of heat. I heard the wind rustling in the clumps of bamboo near the village houses, and the splashing of the little rivulets among the foliage. A cloud of butterflies fluttered above the *tambleang* bushes. It seemed absurd that

Oeroeg was not here. It occurred to me that perceiving this mountain world with my senses was not even possible without Oeroeg's presence. The landscape was not complete without him.

Because of a deep desire to fill this emptiness, I once went to visit Sidris—but there too I had become a stranger. Sidris seemed afraid to address me by my name, as she had been accustomed to doing. She found me too tall, too big to squat on the mat on her front porch. Somebody fetched a rather rickety chair from one of the side rooms, and there I sat, high above Sidris and her housemates. An uneasy feeling took possession of me. Sidris spoke to me in the expressions in the Sundanese language used by an inferior addressing a superior. I would like to have replied using the same forms, but I did not dare for fear she would think I was ridiculing her. Sidris enquired about Oeroeg whom she had not seen for more than two years. She spoke of him in a tone in which I thought I heard pride as well as a kind of sadness. She uttered no word of complaint about his silence and his long absence. I had the feeling that she was now resigned to the fact that Oeroeg had left her and her world for good. I did not stay long at Sidris's. As I descended the path, the image of the surroundings, the rice fields, the green mountain ridges with the clouds above them, etched itself more sharply than ever on my retina, as though a consciousness outside my own predicted that this was the last time I would see all this.

I went to Telaga Hideung too. After Deppoh's death, I had never gone there again. Strange—even in bright daylight it looked as though the lake lay bathed in moonlight. The light that penetrated through the tree-tops and overhanging crowns to the surface of the water was green-gold, as though filtered through stained glass windows. I saw the floating plants, the circles and ripples on the water, at the place where Oeroeg's father had disappeared in the depths. All around in the forest, the silence of noon prevailed. Only the leaves at the very tops of the trees quivered in a light puff of wind. I stared at the shadowy spots in the greenery that I used to think were the hiding-places of Neneh Kombel. I had lost my belief in ghosts years ago, and yet I found the place no less frightening. I knew no name, no definition for this fear, for this feeling of oppression that overcame me whenever I stared at the greenish-black surface of the water. It seemed to me that there were spots in the lake where the water streamed more slowly, where it nearly stood still—in those places the reflection of the trees was dark and dull, the water there impenetrable to light. I stared at those strange, sharply outlined spots, and once I thought I saw, in the depths, a reddish reflex, like blood that was nearly black. A leaf that fluttered down made me leap up, my heart pounding. The lake was hostile, mysterious, a completely unknown element. A cloud passed in front of the sun, and a soft diffused light fell over the surface of the water. I walked quickly down the steep narrow path to the main road, struggling over roots and stones. It was as though something was luring me to look back, but I forced myself not to give in to it. The next day I went back to Batavia.

Oeroeg had completed junior high school with good marks, and had left for Soerabaya. I was just beginning the fourth year of high school. Writing letters, as I could have expected, was not Oeroeg's strongest point. I had to be content with the news I got through Lida. I visited her more frequently now, not so much to hear news of Oeroeg as to find a glimmer of the homeliness that I had come to know in her house in Soekaboemi, a warm and comfortable atmosphere that was entirely lacking at the boarding-school. But Lida was no longer capable of creating that environment. The heat of the tropics as well as the cares that burdened her had made her nervous, and her experiences with guests and with personnel had made her suspicious. Only temporary spells of recovery belied the 'soft soap mentality' that Oeroeg and I, despite our joking, had always secretly valued. The more her *pension* business disappointed her, the greater her expectations with regard to Oeroeg. She showed me a picture of him among his classmates, mostly Indonesian students.

'He looks well, don't you think?' asked Lida, looking at the picture through her needlework spectacles. 'He likes it there, and that doesn't surprise me. He's such a good student. I think it must be nice there in Soerabaya. He lives with Abdullah, with Abdullah's relatives.'

An undertone of longing in her voice made me sit up. Her cheek-bones protruded from her face, now so thin and narrow, her bangs were greyer and as usual stuck to her perspiring forehead. I realized in a flash what she was trying to make me understand. She wanted to go to Soerabaya. That my surmise was correct was proven in the following months. She discussed Oeroeg's letters with me in greater detail. It seemed that he was finding his work more and more interesting, and he had joined a number of organizations, about which he gave no particulars, that took up all his time. I was somewhat surprised by the tone of the letters. I could not easily imagine that it was Oeroeg who had written them, Oeroeg the lover of movies and ice-bars, the imitator of Indo dandies, the intelligent but indifferent student. The letters from Soerabaya reflected entirely different interests. He criticized the government regulations on medicine and hygiene, giving examples of neglect with respect to patients from the lower classes; but he wrote in such a way that I suspected he was using someone else's words, not his own. He had nevertheless registered to become a government-sponsored, so-called 'East Indies doctor', and received an allowance. Once, casually, I spoke of these things to Lida. She replied evasively, 'If mistakes are being made, it's good that he sees them.'

There now ensued a period when fewer letters arrived, and with those she received Lida was less open. She seemed to me to be absent-minded and irritable, oppressed by a problem she was at a loss to know how to solve. Finally, she made the big and bold decision: for the second time she disposed of her *pension* and left with a car full of suitcases and furniture for Soerabaya.

I kept up my contact with Oeroeg and Lida through sporadic letters, now and then a postcard or a hastily written note. I gathered from this correspondence that Abdullah and his family had welcomed Lida into their home. She worked as head nurse in an Indonesian hospital. It was usually she who sent me news. Oeroeg sometimes scribbled his name, or a greeting, under her letter; that was all. The time passed quickly for me; I was studying hard for my final exams. I passed with good marks, as I had expected after all the cramming I did. My father came over to Batavia and we discussed future plans. I was seventeen, nearly eighteen, and tall for my age. The wife of the boarding-school director had seen to it that I was supplied with long pants, since in my too-short shorts, and my

long, hairy legs I looked ridiculous. My father told me his
plans over a glass of beer in the Harmonie Club. He
agreed that I should study engineering, and had decided to
send me to Delft that same year. Everything moved very
quickly now. They booked passage for me on a mail ship,
and a new, freshly painted cabin trunk was ready for me,
filled with my few possessions. Since Eugenie was about to
give birth to her second child, I would not stay at Kebon
Djati before I left. But I did go to Soerabaya to say goodbye to Oeroeg and Lida.

Oeroeg was standing at the station exit, like me wearing
white long pants. His face was thinner than I remembered
it, and its contours were firmer. I noticed almost immediately that he was again wearing his *pici*. He was standing
with one hip lower than the other, his hands on his hip,
staring motionless at the people passing through the bar-
rier. When he saw me, he came up to me slowly and casually to greet me. For a moment, I felt as though I did not
even know him. The smart young boy in his American
linen shoes and striking polo shirt, with his *branie* ways and
his quick sidelong glances in which were hidden shyness as
well as secret ridicule, had been replaced by this serious
young Indonesian, more mature than I, and filled with a
new and this time entirely harmonious self-confidence. At
first, I did not know how to act. We spoke of our studies,
my exams, his school. I asked about his friends and his
activities. He hesitated slightly and then said, 'I have a lot
of contact now with ... with a group ... we all have the
same ideas. There's so much to be done.' I took this to be
an allusion to the organizations he had written about and
asked, 'You wrote once about clubs. What do you do? Do
you have a good time?'

'Oh no, these organizations are not for pleasure. You have the wrong idea. We have no time for that. Of course, we enjoy ourselves too,' he added.

'Don't you dance any more?' I asked teasingly. His face darkened, and there was not even a hint of a smile. 'There is so much to be done,' he repeated.

The small carriage that we had taken at the station drew up in front of an old East Indies house in a quiet tree-lined street. The front veranda was hardly visible behind a great number of pots of various sizes full of ferns and palms, which stood on the balustrade and the low wall. From the darkness of the inner room emerged a woman in a loose, flowered cotton dress, her feet in slippers, her grey hair combed smoothly back, and fastened on each side with hairpins. Her walk reflected unmistakably the way people in the Indies moved. It was Lida.

'Hello,' she said, with a trace of her old, fresh smile. She stroked her forehead and invited me to come in. At the back of the house sat Abdullah and his relatives: a stout elderly man in pyjamas, two girls of about sixteen, with fine Javanese features. Abdullah had changed less than Oeroeg. He greeted me with a smile and pushed a rocking chair towards me. The conversation was stilted. Neither Oeroeg, nor Lida, nor I could recover the old familiar tone of the past. I sensed that this would never be possible again. I could not identify this Lida, slumping in her chair, with her slippers hanging loose on her bare feet, breaking some candied tamarind into pieces, with the woman I had known in Soekaboemi and later in Batavia. It was a mystery to me why she was living in this house. There was no shortage of housing in Soerabaya, and there could easily have been another way for her to be near Oeroeg. The back veranda, with its old-fashioned furniture, was filled with cages in which a whole variety of twittering birds were jumping up and down. A *beo* (myna) perched on a pole with a thin chain around its foot. Here too there were innumerable ferns and other plants in porcelain pots. The back garden was dark, almost entirely covered with a dome of pendulous leaves and the air roots of a *waringin* (banyan) tree. I know it sounds strange, but for a moment it seemed to me that there was some connection between this shadowy back veranda full of plants and trees and Telaga Hideung as I had seen it when a cloud passed in front of the sun. The impression only partly disappeared when one of Abdullah's nieces lighted a lamp, a bare frosted sphere, at once surrounded by a swarm of insects.

After the evening meal, the tone of the conversation became a bit more pleasant. Lida told me, speaking with a tedious slowness that I was not accustomed to, about her job in the hospital. I asked her why she was not working in a European hospital. She exchanged glances with Oeroeg and Abdullah, which I could not understand.

'She speaks fluent Malay now', said Oeroeg, 'and she's learning Javanese.'

'To help Oeroeg when he starts working among the people', added Lida, without taking her eyes off her foster son.

'Later—that will be necessary later,' said Oeroeg, with a flicker of a smile.

'Oh—so you'll be working for the government,' I said, not so much to hear an affirmative reply as to lead the conversation into a course of ideas that I could follow. Abdullah, who was shelling peanuts, jerked his head up.

'No,' said Oeroeg. 'I'm not going to work for the government.'

'But they're giving you an allowance, aren't they? Or not?' I suggested.

'She's paying for my studies,' said Oeroeg, moving his head to the side in Lida's direction. I looked from the one to the other. The insects rustled and droned around the lamp. The old man, who had said little up to now, rocked silently back and forth in his chair. Lida fiddled with a splinter of bamboo on the edge of the table. But Oeroeg and Abdullah answered my glance. I suddenly had the feeling that this was the moment they had been waiting for for a long time. They wanted to lay open their cards to an opponent. At that instant, I was the symbol, the personification of what they were launching an offensive against with all their being. I forced myself to hold on to the sense of reality that was threatening to escape me on this quiet back veranda.

'What do you mean?' I asked Oeroeg.

'That I don't want to have anything to do with the Dutch government,' he replied evenly. 'I don't need your help.'

'Our help?' I retorted, and I flushed with anger, for now the significance of his words had come home to me. 'You certainly have something to do with Lida!'

'Lida thinks the same way we do,' said Oeroeg proudly. One thing led to another, and to a debate in which I had to take a defensive attitude, since the whole matter was strange to me. I knew little or nothing of the nationalistic current, about the schools set up by the nationalists and therefore not acknowledged by the colonial government; about the ferment that was taking place in certain layers of

Indonesian society. I listened in silence to the torrent of accusations and reproaches that they now, all aflame, directed against the government, against the Dutch, against white people in general. I believed that many of their claims were not well founded, or unjust, but I had no arguments at my disposal that I could use to refute them. My surprise increased by the minute, since Oeroeg, in his new milieu of progressive students and young agitators, had become an orator.

'The villagers, the common people, have purposely been kept stupid,' he said fiercely, looking straight at me as he leaned over the table. 'It was in your interest to prevent the people from developing. But that's over now. We will see to that. They need no *wayang* puppets and no *gamelan* and none of their superstitions and medicine men—we no longer live in the kingdom of Mataram, and Java need not resemble a picture on a postcard for tourists. We don't need all that ballast. The Borobudur is only a pile of old stones. Let them give us factories and warships and modern clinics and schools, and a say in our own affairs. . . .'

As Oeroeg sat there arguing, emphasizing his words with his clenched left fist, I saw the staring faces of the others around me as though in a dream. In a shadowy corner of the back veranda, outside the circle of light made by the lamp, Abdullah's nieces were whispering to each other. Again and again the old man nodded approvingly. Abdullah continued shelling his peanuts, but when he looked up I saw his eyes sparkling behind his spectacles. Now and then Lida came out with a 'Yes . . . yes'. She had succeeded in getting the bamboo splinter loose, and was busy splitting it into thin fibres with her finger-nail. She never once looked at me. I had the feeling that in her heart she was embarrassed for me, and that in the depths of her soul she was perhaps aware that this new ideal was the last leap to safety of her lonely childlike spirit. I had an intense feeling of sympathy for her. If I had been able to formulate all these things more sharply for myself, everything might have turned out differently. I sat opposite Oeroeg and Abdullah with the sensation that I was playing a part in a bad dream. This sense of unreality did not disappear later when I went to sleep in a room they had prepared for me. Through the wide open windows, I saw the stars twinkling behind the branches of the *waringin* tree. All around me were the numberless familiar sounds of the East Indian night. But I was an outsider. In the adjoining room, I heard Abdullah and Oeroeg talking in muffled voices. The separation between their world and mine was complete.

Return

I left for Europe. There is no point here in writing at length on the period that followed, about my short visit to my mother in Nice, my studies in Delft which were discontinued because of the war and later, because of measures taken by the Germans, completely stopped. I too had a share in underground activities like most of my acquaintances. I thought often of the fate that might have befallen Oeroeg and Lida, my father and his family, a fate that I could do no more than imagine. After Japan's capitulation, I received some news. My father was dead. Eugenie and the children were waiting in Batavia to be transported to Holland. I heard nothing about Oeroeg and Lida, even though I tried through various channels to obtain information about them. I completed my studies and then did what I had been planning to do for years: I applied for a job in the Indies. The chaotic situation there, the strange relationships that the Japanese Occupation had left behind, did not daunt me. I had not a moment's doubt that these difficulties would be of a temporary nature. The 'colonial' way of thinking—so often critized in my country after the war, whether or not unjustifiably—was alien to me. My desire to return to the Indies and to work there was based mainly on a deeply rooted feeling of belonging to the country where I had been born and brought up. The years in Holland, important as they were, meant less to me than my youth and my school days there.

If it is true that for every human being there is a land-scape of the spirit, a certain atmosphere, an environment that awakens responsive vibrations in the furthest recesses of his being, then my landscape was—and is—the moun-tain slopes of the Priangan: the bitter fragrance of the tea plants, the splashing of clear streams over rocks, the blue shadows of clouds over the lowland. That my longing for all of this could be poignant I had realized during the years in which every contact and any return was impossible. The meeting with Eugenie in the Hague, her violent and hysterical rejection of that faraway country full of horrors, could not quench my joy at returning.

I arrived in Batavia at the same time as the breaking out of what, for purposes of simplification, I shall call the 'op-eration to restore Dutch rule'. I found no trace of Oeroeg. There was no information on the fate of the medical college students. In the streets of Batavia, now more disordered than before, but still familiar to me, as a well-known face, disfigured by suffering and old age, can still be recognized, I automatically tried to find Oeroeg among the passers-by.

A hundred times, I thought I saw him, and just as often, looking more closely, was I disappointed. Once I saw Abdullah in a crowd around the Aneta Press Office when a communiqué was being issued. I recognized him from his spectacles, although he looked shabby and was much thinner. I called out 'Abdullah?' over the heads of the people that separated us. He looked up and around. Did he see me? The sunlight glittered in his spectacles so that I could not follow his gaze. He stood still a moment among the pushing crowd, with his face turned towards me. I wanted to walk up to him, but before I could reach him, he passed me in the other direction at a distance of several metres. I called him again, in my haste shoving the by-standers aside; but Abdullah had already disappeared in the throng.

*   *   *

My job involved the repair of bridges destroyed by the republicans in the Priangan. My first post was only a few hours' drive from Kebon Djati, and I could not resist the temptation, at the first opportunity to go along with an inspection patrol that was proceeding in that direction. Standing in the open truck, I looked out over the beloved landscape. On either side of the road full of pot-holes were the same green slopes, the same clumps of bamboo that I remembered from the past. The water in the rice fields sparkled in the sunlight, and reflected not only the clouds sailing across the sky in unchanging tranquility, but the telephone poles as well, some of them hanging askew, others cut down, in a tangled net of loose wires. Groups of people, with dirty rags around their bodies, stared after the truck with expressionless faces. Only the small children jumped up and down on the side of the road, their shrill voices still audible above the rumbling of our wheels. The station where Oeroeg and I used to board the train to Soekaboemi was only a floor plan of blackened stones. Weeds and bushes grew where once the *warung* had stood, and the village houses on the other side of the road had disappeared. We came to a bend in the road, and I knew that we would now drive into the lanes leading out of the tea gardens. From this point, the house of the administrator used to be visible, higher up on the slope, a white spot among the endless rows of tea plants. I leaned over the side of the truck and my heart beat faster. I knew that I could not expect to find the old image intact, since Kebon Djati had lain on the route of the retreating republicans. But no matter how neglected and dilapidated the plantation might be, I had come home.

The landscape that stretched out before me by the bend in the road was a scene I would not even have seen in a nightmare. The blackened crests of the hills were bare: desolate, ghostlike. The truck drove up along the road as though it was wending its way between the ribs of a giant cadaver. When I realized that I had forgotten to look at the house, I knew at the same moment that it was no longer there. It would even have been difficult for me to point out the place where it should have been.

The driver of the truck offered to take us to the ruins. The patrol had been here before to determine the damage. But I refused, and we went further, among the black hills. It was not until we had forced our way into the tunnel of the forest that I found again the surroundings I had retained in my memory. The same ice-cold rivulets seeped down along the steep walls overgrown with ferns; the same smell of earth and rotting plants met us out of the dusky depths among the green. I recognized the spot where the path to Telaga Hideung must be hidden in the wilderness, and I asked the others to stop, a suggestion they welcomed after the long ride. They jumped out of the truck to stretch their legs. Under a pretext, I managed to leave them, and I ducked away among the trees. I walked quickly, although the path was hardly recognizable under the dense growth. I looked up into the tree-tops, and towards the light spot between the leaves in the distance where I knew that the sunlight streamed down to the lake through the ravine above. Birds whose names I had forgotten sang all around me, hidden among the foliage. The forest was still full of the mysterious, unceasing rustling that will forever belong uniquely to this spot. The lake too, black and shining, the water plants, and the ripples the wind made on the surface—I found them all unchanged. A wood-pigeon called, sweetly and enticingly, in the dark grove of trees on the other side. I sat on my heels at the water's edge and gazed at the twinkling green-golden crowns of the trees, with the sun shedding its light on them in the upper reaches of the ravine. There was hardly a sound in the water, where a lizard shot away among the plants on the bank. The aerial roots of the trees appeared to be floating motionless on the surface of the water. Again the wood-pigeon called, closer by now, it seemed. I thought back to the time when Oeroeg and I, in our striped playsuits, played on the steps of the back veranda of Kebon Djati. The cooing of the pigeons in their cages hanging behind the servants' rooms had never ceased.

The grass on the edge of the lake rustled in the wind, and again there were ripples on the water. I thought I saw the dull red sheen under the surface that years back had reminded me of clotted blood. On the back porch at Abdullah's, I had thought of it too—why? I wondered.

A shadow fell on the ground beside me. I turned round and saw an Indonesian, in dirty khaki shorts, with a head-cloth of batik material wound sloppily around his dishevelled hair. He shot a fierce, blind glance at me, and signalled that I should hold my hands above my head under threat of the revolver. 'Oeroeg,' I said in an undertone. The wood pigeon flew out of the trees flapping its wings.

I do not know how long we stood there facing each other, neither one of us saying a word. I waited, completely without fear, fully at ease. It seemed to me then that all the events of our lives, from the time of Oeroeg's and my births, had irrevocably led to this moment. It had begun to grow in us, had ripened, outside our wills, outside our consciousness. This was the very first time, this was the juncture at which we could meet each other in complete honesty.

He raised his weapon. 'I'm not alone,' I said, although I do not believe it was fear that made me say it. I really did not care at that moment whether he shot me or not. The expression of his face remained unchanged, but he released his forefinger from the cock of the revolver, which made me conclude that he was alone.

'Go away,' he said in Sundanese. 'Go away, otherwise I'll shoot. You have no business here.'

I saw that he had turned pale. A scar on his cheek stood out against his skin more sharply than before.

'Listen,' I began, but he interrupted me with fury in his voice. 'Go away! You have no business being here!'

His eyes gleamed like the water of Telaga Hideung, just as reluctant to reveal what lay in the depths. I realized that it would be insanity to try to tempt him to speak. What I *could* discover was clearly visible. Around his right arm was a dirty rag on which the mark of the red cross could still be seen. The kris in his belt, the *kain* (cloth) wound round his head Sundanese-style—his khaki shorts, American fashion, and his revolver, perhaps inherited from the Japanese—what more was there to learn about the stages through which he had passed?

'Go away!' he repeated—but he needn't have said it. I turned half-round and looked at Telaga Hideung, ancient crater that the rain had turned into a lake—a mirror for trees and clouds, a playground for light and shadow, gusts of wind, and water snakes, the hidden kingdom that betrayed its impersonal cruelty in the presence of blood and plants that clutched you under its black surface. A cloud passed in front of the sun and there was a cold gloss over the lake, like ink and lead. The sharp tones of a patrol whistle sounded in the distance. I had been missed.

His eyes searched round the wood with lightning speed. He was no longer thinking of me. Every muscle of his body was strained in defence, in flight. He stood, half turned away from me, as though deliberating with himself. The tendons of his neck and his thin shoulder-blades were visible through the tears in his shirt. He was at the same time pitiful and terrifying—the hunted in ambush, but with the intelligence that had destroyed villages and scorched hills. For one more moment, I watched him standing there, against the dark background of the forest. The voices of my fellow-travellers were not far away, on the path between the trees. I looked around, but he had already disappeared, and I did not know which way he had gone. The leaves hardly moved; it could have been the wind that caused them to quiver so. I walked back and joined the patrol. Was it really Oeroeg? I do not know, and I never will. I have even lost the ability to recognize him.

All I have really wanted to do is put down in words an account of the youth we spent together. I want to fix those years that have disappeared without a trace as though they were never more than smoke in the wind. Kebon Djati is a memory; so is the boarding-school, and Lida. Abdullah and I pass each other in silence; and Oeroeg—I shall never meet him again. It is superfluous to admit that I did not understand him. I knew him as I knew Telaga Hideung— as the sparkling surface of a crater lake. But I never fathomed the depths. Is it too late? Am I forever to be a stranger in the land of my birth, on the earth from which I do not wish to be transplanted? Only time will tell.

Lidah Boeaja (Crocodile's Tongue)

ALOË FEROX, Lidah Boeaja (Mal.) Treelike plant having rosette of leaves with jagged edges set with sharp hook.... On the island of Java cultivated as an ornamental plant.... The juice from the leaves is used as shampoo.

(*Netherlands Indies Encyclopedia*)

MRS YAMADA stood in the backyard and gazed at the prickly, fleshy-leaved plant Lidah Boeaja, man's height in its bed surrounded with white bricks. She would have preferred to have the plant dug up, but the ladies who lived in the annexe, the widow Matulaka from Ambon (from whom Mr Yamada had rented the house) and her friend Non du Cloux, used the whitish slimy juice of the leaves to wash their hair. Mrs Yamada knew now that she would never be able to change that stony piece of ground and the wilderness of shrubs into the kind of garden she had had in Nagoya. She missed the peonies, the azaleas, the dwarf pine with its parasol of dense, dark green needles, and especially the pond full of carp that swam to the surface whenever she came to the edge to feed them. From that spot, she could see a chain of mountains rising in the distance; and a fresh breeze from the sea came blowing over the Bay of Isenumi.

After their departure from Japan, her husband had wished her to adapt herself as much as possible to the Western customs of Batavia. Mr Yamada had a 'Hairdressing Salon for Gentlemen', as announced on a signboard near the garden wall. Through the open swing-doors of the three entrances that opened on to the front veranda, you could admire from the street the interior of the salon: solid dressing-tables with marble tops, mirrors in frames with Jugenstil motifs of green and blue irises, chairs with adjustable head supports. Flacons full of red and purple liquid were ranged on racks along the wall. There were posters of Piver: nymphs and cherubs scattering roses, wreathed with rings of smoke from fragrant offerings. Mr Yamada found that these sugary embellishments gave his hairdressing salon a real Western allure. Even when there were no customers, he walked back and forth in a white jacket, his hair matchlessly trimmed and mirror-smooth from brilliantine. He wore a pair of black-rimmed spectacles because they were so flattering to him; optically, the lenses were useless. There were few prospective customers for a haircut or a shave. Was it because of the quiet run-down street, or did the salon not look Western enough? Mr Yamada seemed not to be upset over the fact, to the amazement of the ladies in the annexe, who had great difficulty making ends meet from the sale of their home-made delicacies. They sometimes felt disturbed by the unconcern of the Japanese, who, light-hearted and smiling, kept himself busy in his empty salon—he dusted the furniture, cleaned the mirrors, arranged the scissors and bottles. They felt perturbed, not because of him (even though he was a dandy and extremely polite, they disliked him intensely), but for the sake of Mrs Yamada, that exquisite little lady with waxen face and hair piled up high on her head, a real doll. They felt sorry for her, and loved to speculate about the secrets of her home life.

'Those Japs!' said Non du Cloux often, as she kneaded tamarind cookies (Mrs Matulaka keeping her company as she munched on snacks). 'These Japs, they treat their wives like slaves. This one treats his very badly.'

'Ah, how do you know? mumbled Mrs Matulaka, her mouth full of sweets. Her expression of caution and doubt was intentional, since she knew that Non's speculations, in response to her feigned soberness, would be even bolder. 'How can you say that, Non? What do you know about the Japanese?'

'I have my eyes all about me—what do you think?' Non moved her head in the direction of the hedge of spiraea between the annexe and the big house. Parts of the wild, rank-growing mass of green with pale clusters of flowers were sagging, leaving openings that allowed a view of the back veranda and the yard of the Yamadas. They did see something; they did hear something, albeit not much. Mr Yamada, always smiling and bowing to strangers, put on a hard face and struck a commanding, even snappish tone when he spoke to his wife. Mrs Yamada was silent and preserved her subdued, obsequious attitude full of gentle grace. She was mostly alone. On her straw sandals, she shuffled lightly and quickly through the veranda or along the tiled, roofed path to the outbuildings. The Yamadas had no servants. Mrs Yamada did the cooking as well as the laundry, to the dismay of the Mesdames Matulaka and du Cloux, who even in a period of an acute shortage of money, would not have dreamed of not having a servant. Every morning Mrs Yamada hung her wash out to dry, stretching up on her toes to reach the line. Under the edge of her kimono, her white cotton socks were visible and her sleeves fell far back on her arms. The Yamadas had fallen on difficult days; the neighbours were convinced of it, when a smaller sign appeared beside the large one near the gate: 'E. Yamada, Ladies' and Children's Fashions'. Every day now the whirring of a sewing-machine could be heard from one of the side rooms; and cuttings of cloth and tiny balls of thread appeared here and there in the garden. Mrs Yamada was very seldom seen now in the garden and on the tiled path, although she washed and cooked as dutifully as ever. She looked tired, found the spectators behind the hedge. Above the kitchen-table, full of dough and spicy sauces, harsh words were spoken about Mr Yamada, who played the gentleman in his empty salon while she worked herself to death. For Mrs Yamada clearly had more success with her enterprise than her husband with his. Customers came for fittings until late in the evening; ladies' bicycles stood in the rack that had originally been set up for the vehicles of the gentlemen who were to have been trimmed and shaved by Mr Yamada. Dogcarts and taxis often waited in front of the gate. Mrs Yamada employed two assistants, the Nogushi sisters, as slight and slender as small children. They were the daughters of a business friend of Mr Yamada's, a guest who came nearly every day, and the only one who visited the salon for a shave and a haircut. The arrival of the two girls did indeed provide relief for Mrs Yamada.

Occasionally, as at this moment, she found a moment to go outside. But the heat in the garden was oppressive, and the unkempt plants and shrubs, especially the Lidah Boeaja, with its sharp spikes, filled her with disgust. That morning Mrs Matulaka had cut off a leaf in two places. The juice had not yet congealed, and gleamed on the scars in the thick leathery fibre. From the street and the adjoining yards, and from the encroaching kampong all around, behind trees and fences of wattlework, arose a variety of sounds: the cackling of chickens, the shouting of people quarreling, a man's voice telling a story, accompanied by the laughter of a group of listeners; in the annexe someone was grinding spices in a mortar, with in the background the vague din of the traffic in the city, coming to life again after the noon siesta. To present some semblance of activity—she was aware of the interest in her behind the hedge—Mrs Yamada carried a few dishes into the kitchen and a pitcher of water to the back veranda. For a moment she saw, in the dark interior, the movement of Mr Yamada's white coat. There was a stripe of light when he opened the door to the salon; and then darkness.

*   *   *

Etsu Asama was nineteen years of age when she and Yamada were married. Her father had modern ideas—Etsu had learned to read and write and sew at a school where Western dress was compulsory: white blouse, short black skirt, hair in plaits. At home, her mother preserved the old traditions. Not for a Japanese the decadent boldness, the nonchalance of the West; no more beautiful jewel, no more effective weapon than silence; be docile, but attentive; self-control means power. Etsu very soon understood the art of being decorative like a flower, concealing her own desires and opinions behind a mask as smooth as porcelain. Mr Yamada was from Kobe, where his father sold cosmetic articles. He aspired to greater heights. He became private secretary to the manager of a Nagoya aircraft factory. Etsu's father had met Yamada at a reception. He invited him to his home and introduced him to his wife and daughter. Did Yamada fall in love with the quiet girl who served with such dexterity and grace, and later, while the gentlemen conversed, sat modestly at a distance, looking beautiful? Was Etsu impressed by the intelligent self-confident young man in his modern suit? The marriage negotiations proceeded smoothly and according to tradition.

They lived in Nagoya, far from the smoke of the factories, in the area of Yamada's employer famed for its landscaping. Mr Yamada was usually absent all day, often in the evenings as well, and always a few days at a time. Etsu accepted and obeyed her husband, as she had been taught to do. She was not unhappy. She had indeed observed that there were two Yamadas. In company, among strangers, Mr Yamada was lively and affable, all smiles; he bestowed the greatest care on his clothes and appearance. But when he was at home alone with Etsu, he seemed to change: he wandered around languidly, preferably in his short sleeping kimono; he wanted to be served, spoke little, read the papers, gazed from the veranda over the sloping garden at the bay and the peninsula in the distance. Now and then, he went through piles of papers that he had brought home in his always carefully locked briefcase. He covered the characters with his hand in an ostensibly unobtrusive manner when Etsu was in his vicinity. She glided through the rooms in her stockinged feet, the padded hem of her kimono barely rustling over the mats. With eyes downcast, she served her husband food and drink. Every evening, she soundlessly unfolded the two draught-screens and spread the mattresses out behind them. Then she knelt by her toilet-case, and one by one removed the pins and combs from her hair. Jet-black and feathery, the loose strands fell over her breast and shoulders, a transformation which never failed to attract Yamada's desirous attention.

Etsu remained childless, which made her even more silent. Mr Yamada was now often impatient and irritable, and made it clear to her that it was only due to his kindness that she could fulfil her role as lady of the house. But he did not mention divorce. He took her along to Batavia, where, he told her completely unexpectedly, he wanted to open a hairdressing salon with equipment supplied by his father. Etsu showed no surprise. She packed their bags, and took leave of her family. On board, when Yamada retreated to the cabin to go through his papers, Etsu sat on deck, her kimono folded tightly about her legs to keep out the wind, and stared at the dark green water marbled with foam-crested waves that rose and fell alongside.

In Batavia it had been difficult for her to become accustomed to the heat and the humidity and to the somewhat dilapidated house in a narrow street on the border of the lower town. She learned Malay words out of books that her husband brought home for her. Since he continually warned her against the overtures of Mrs Matulaka and Ms du Cloux, Etsu kept herself at a distance. If she had so desired, she could have had a *baboe*. But the women in the neighbourhood who offered their services as housemaids looked slovenly and had a bad reputation. Etsu preferred to do all her work herself. She kept the tiled floors scrupulously clean, and dusted the European furniture that Mr Yamada had chosen at an auction. In the cool of the early morning, she bought their daily necessities at a nearby market.

After some time, Yamada introduced her to other Japanese, to his business relation Noguchi and his family, and to the Okamuras. The Okamuras had a well-patronized shop in the city centre where they sold toys and knick-knacks. In the beginning, Etsu enjoyed visiting the long narrow shop illuminated by coloured lamps, where dolls, lacquered boxes, vases, and tea services were so tightly packed that one had to edge sideways along the counters. Anything and everything was available at Okamura's, from suspenders to Satsuma porcelain. There was a sweetish smell that reminded Etsu of Nagoya. She walked through the shop, occasionally purchasing a small article, a box, a gilded comb, a miniature temple gate, varnished red, in which a tiny clock swung back and forth. Mr Okamura usually sat in a small office behind the shop, among cash-books, piles of wood-wool, and empty boxes. It was a stuffy place, in spite of the electric fan. In the shop, Mrs Okamura held sway: small and thin, with a skull-like head. At first sight, an inconquerable antipathy arose between her and Etsu Yamada. Yet Etsu continued to visit the shop regularly, attracted by the familiar fragrance, the profusion of things Japanese. Because Yamada desired it, they paid a few visits to the Okamuras at home, and in turn received them on the inner veranda behind the salon. On these occasions, Etsu met Asuko, the Okamuras' daughter. Etsu disliked the mother, but the daughter filled her with fear. As a child, she had heard stories of women who at night changed into bloodthirsty foxes; they were of rare beauty, but a careful look revealed that there was something in their eyes and lips that betrayed their true nature. To Etsu, Asuko resembled one of those demons in the fairy-tale. Asuko's mouth was narrow and dark red. Often, when she smiled, baring her small sharp teeth, Yamada's eyes lighted up with the same look that Etsu had seen in them on the quiet evenings in Nagoya when she let down her hair.

Yamada's friend Noguchi had a fishing business in the lower city; his prows sailed out along the coast and among the islands in the Bay of Batavia. Mrs Noguchi was good-natured and stupid: Etsu had little to do with her. Yamada never told her how he and Noguchi had first met each other. They held long conversations, in muffled voices, when Noguchi came for a shave, and in the evenings on the inner veranda as well, behind closed doors. Etsu was quickly aware that her presence was not desired. The distance between her and her husband was so great that she now asked him no questions. Since their arrival in Batavia, he had no longer touched her. During the short afternoon siesta, and at night, in the big bed with the *klamboe*, he turned his back on her as a matter of course.

One day, deviating from her usual custom, Etsu did her daily shopping late in the afternoon. She did not like the crowded shopping district and hurried home through the narrow untidy streets. A dogcart rode by, in which sat Yamada with Noguchi and Asuko Okamura. They were leaning against each other talking excitedly. As far as Etsu knew, the Okamuras and the Noguchis had never met each other. Several days later, the Yamadas again visited the Okamuras. The two men sat some distance away from the women and were discussing the news in the Japanese newspapers that had just come out. Mrs Okamura and Asuko were talking to Etsu Yamada. Etsu casually mentioned the name Noguchi. Mother and daughter asked in surprise who that might be and wanted to know further details about this fellow countryman who was unknown to them. Smiling, Mrs Yamada complied with their request.

She now understood too why it was necessary for her to help earn their livelihood, although she had never noticed that her husband had a shortage of money. Without proof of a source of income, they could be expelled from the country. She did not regard this as a threat—on the contrary, she desired nothing more than to return to Nagoya or to her parents. But Mr Yamada said he had to stay, and therefore she resigned herself to her fate. In a very short time, her sewing brought in more income than what was absolutely essential. She worked meticulously, conscientiously, and promptly, and thereby acquired a good name. She was overwhelmed with orders. The bills were made out and payments collected by Mr Yamada, whose hairdressing salon now fulfilled only a decorative function.

When Mr Yamada was out, Etsu sometimes entered this fragrant sanctuary, after having carefully closed the swing-doors. She held the bottles in her hand and smelled them with a repugnant grimace. She opened the drawers of the dressing-tables where the shining scissors and hair-clippers were neatly arranged. She studied the Piver posters attentively.

In general, Mrs Yamada disliked her customers. She liked the Indo-Europeans best, although the mixed blood, the indeterminate race, was strange to her. The Dutch women were all alike in their self-assurance, their lack of tact. When they were reserved, they gave the impression of being offensively haughty; to Etsu, there was something immodest in their friendliness. They talked too loud and too much; they knew no nuances of courtesy. She was fond of only one of them, a certain Mrs Van der Vlecke.

She was never obtrusive nor condescending, nor did she have that pale freckled skin and nondescript hair colour that Etsu found repugnant; her smell was not unpleasant either. She often brought her children with her, and Mrs Yamada made clothes and underwear for them. Once she happened to lift the smallest boy off the chair on which he had been standing when being fitted. She was forced to cast down her eyes to conceal the emotion that overcame her when she touched the little firm warm body. It was not jealousy. When the children left, she always slipped something into their hands, hastily and without smiling: a doll's paper parasol, some artistic trifle, all from Okamura's shop. From other customers who inquisitively watched Mrs Van der Vlecke's car drive away, Etsu heard—without asking—that Mr Van der Vlecke was a 'bigwig', an important person in one of the government departments. This fact did not become of significance to her until she noticed how exuberant her husband and his friend Noguchi were when they heard that it was his wife who came to Etsu for her sewing.

At this time, Mrs Yamada was so busy that she very seldom met the Okamuras (which she did not regret). Yamada now visited them nearly every day, preferably in the evening hours. It was usual for Etsu to have been in bed a long time when her husband finally crept silently under the mosquito netting. Eventually it seemed that a visit was unavoidable. Etsu knew that it was expected of her, and she did not wish to be found lacking in courtesy. One afternoon she dressed herself with care, spread rice powder over her forehead and cheeks and rode in a *sado* to the Okamura's shop. Mr Okamura was sitting in his office, as usual, under the fan that brought no relief from the heat.

The siesta hour was not yet over, and Mrs Okamura stood in the now empty shop. She bowed, but her smile was full of triumph and contempt. They exchanged compliments in soft voices. In the shadow of the back of the house, between the screens and the porcelain vases that reached a man's height, Asuko now appeared, drawing her kimono tightly over her pregnant belly. She greeted Etsu from afar.

With a straight face, Mrs Okamura told Etsu that Asuko would soon return to Japan. She was needed there. It was no longer necessary for her to teach the children of Japanese families in Batavia whom she had so devotedly initiated into the traditions of Nippon. But, ah, Mrs Yamada would not be interested, not having any children of her own. And moreover, was it not so that she had little interest in the things that were so dear to the hearts of the Okamuras and her husband Mr Yamada as well: the fame and honour and greatness of the holy fatherland, so strikingly symbolized in the sign of the Rising Sun? Mrs Okamura excused herself for being so tactless as to annoy her guest by speaking of personal matters; she began to talk about the heat that had recently been so damp and close, and about a newly arrived shipment of silk for obi sashes.

That evening, Mr Yamada remained at home. For the first time in many months, he spoke to his wife at great length. They sat together on the inner veranda. The only lamp, screened by a white frosted glass shade, cast a chill light over the furniture, the plastered walls, the shining head of Mr Yamada. Etsu sat erect, her feet prettily close together. Her eyes followed the movements of the small house lizards that darted over the walls snapping at insects. The crickets droned in the long grass of the front garden. Further away, on the street, the tinkling of an ice-cream vendor's bell could be heard. From the annexe came stifled laughter. Non du Cloux and Mrs Matulaka had a visitor, a cultivator of herbs who also practised as a clairvoyant. The three of them loved to sit around a small table-lamp and occupy themselves with all sorts of secret and gruesome mysteries.

Mr Yamada announced to his wife that he was thinking of going to Japan for an indefinite period of time. Etsu could now take care of herself. Noguchi would manage her income and as main tenant, move in with his family. If Etsu's status had to be changed, she could register as a member of the Noguchi family.

'Is this all clear to you?' asked Mr Yamada. Etsu replied in the affirmative. She understood fully. Once, in her grandmother's house, there had been a woman, an unmarried sister of her mother's, who worked from early in the morning until late at night in exchange for the protection of a place to live. Mr Yamada continued speaking. He had reserved a cabin on the *Osaka Maru*. Etsu only nodded. She knew from her conversation with Mrs Okamura that the pregnant Asuko was also returning to the holy fatherland Nippon on the same ship.

Mrs Yamada sat in the shade of the roof on the steps of the back veranda. At this time of afternoon, there was usually a cooler breeze to be felt. As always, she busied herself with a variety of little jobs: she arranged spools of thread and rolls of tape in a box, embroidered a monogram, or sewed on buttons. She leaned against the side wall of the veranda, even though it was uncomfortable. Half a metre above the ground, a shabby-looking whitewashed water-pipe ran like a horizontal scar over the wall. On the inner veranda, the conduit pipes branched out into a network of curves and thicknesses. When Mr Yamada furnished the hair-dressing salon, he had had new pipes installed leading to his washstands.

The long frayed leaves of the banana trees in the yard against the fence gleamed in the afternoon light. Past the hedge of the annexe, Mrs Matulaka appeared, in a peignoir, with wet hair shining from the juice of the Lidah Boeaja. She hung a bath-towel out to dry on the line, and waved to Etsu. The machines of the Noguchi girls whirred in the sewing-room.

About half past four, Etsu heard the crunching of the gravel in the front yard under wagon wheels. She was aware that her husband had called a dogcart from the front veranda and was now going out. She waited a moment, stood up, and walked to the salon. One of Noguchi's daughters, who needed a roll of silk, saw her standing there, wrapping something up. Mrs Yamada asked the girls to continue working until she came back; she had to go out, but would not be long. In the street, she thought she saw Noguchi in the distance. She put up her parasol and took a narrow path that led along garden walls and the kampong to a parallel road.

Noguchi was surprised that Mrs Yamada was not at home; she never liked to go out at that time of day. His daughters knew only that she had sat on the back steps for a while and that she had later gone out with a small package in her hand. Noguchi spoke then about the coming changes, about the family's move. The girls knew. They followed their father to the veranda and knelt beside him on the mat where Etsu had sat, from where they could look over their new domain: the tiled roofed path, the outbuildings, the ill-kept backyard. They wanted an aviary there for parrots and wood-pigeons.

Through an opening in the spiraea hedge, Mrs Matulaka appeared, a towel wound round her head like a turban and a flowered piece of clothing over her arm. She often managed to enter the Yamadas' house by pretending to bring something to be mended. At first, she was disappointed to find her neighbour not at home; but since a conversation with Noguchi, whom she had often seen from a distance, could provide material for discussion with her friend du Cloux, she agreed that the helpful girls should put her torn dress under the sewing-machine needle. She herself dropped down beside Noguchi on the steps. She spoke to him as she usually did to his daughters and Mrs Yamada, very loudly and slowly. She could coax no more out of him than a nod of the head and polite, but extremely brief replies. Non du Cloux, who stood watching behind the foliage of the hedge, was highly annoyed. She clacked with her tongue. That Toos Matulaka ... so stupid. He is not even listening, the fat Jap.

Finally, Mrs Matulaka hoisted herself up, holding on to the water-pipe.

'When I used to live here, I always called this my telephone,' she said, turning to the Noguchi daughters, who had repaired the torn hem. The girls giggled as always at everything Mrs Matulaka said. They found her irresistibly comical, with her dark brown face, in which the whites of her eyes and her teeth shone so conspicuously.

'Yes, my telephone,' continued the Ambonese, of the opinion that the laughter was for her remark. 'Listen, all of you. Wait now. Keep those things quiet.' She waved in the direction of the sewing-machines.

'Just listen, sir. Look. This way,' gesturing to explain. Noguchi had only to move his head slightly to rest his ear against the opening of the pipe. Mrs Matulaka walked to the inner veranda. She closed the doors, after having raised her forefinger secretively.

A few seconds later, Noguchi heard a strange sound in the conduit: the voice of Mrs Matulaka, distorted into an underground drone, as though of a doll, a dwarf. Sometimes it seemed to recede, then it swelled up. Straining slightly, he could understand every word of her monologue, as she walked back and forth on the inner veranda. The Noguchi girls, who heard nothing, but who saw their father's face turn ashen, came quickly closer, and squatted behind him against the wall. They burst out laughing and clapped their hands, but were shocked into silence by a sign from Noguchi. Mrs Matulaka reappeared.

'Now, what did I tell you? It's a telephone, isn't it?' she asked triumphantly, and she told how she had discovered this rare phenomenon after the water-pipes had been installed: she was sitting here, in the exact same spot, enjoying the cool of the evening, and then she had suddenly heard, through the pipe, what her husband, who was still living then, was saying to someone on the inner veranda! Noguchi stood up, bowed properly, and brushed past her inside.

So a great deal of what he had discussed with Yamada during his visits here might be known to Etsu, whom he had often seen recently sitting on the steps of the back veranda. Did she know, then, about the letters, the instructions whose purpose was to provide information to Nippon's outposts? Did she know about the spoils that Noguchi's fishing prows brought along from their trips: descriptions and designations of the military fortifications along the coast? She must have caught names of her countrymen who had ensconced themselves on Java and other parts of the archipelago as barbers, shopkeepers, and photographers. She probably knew too that Asuko Okamura had long been one of the most valuable of their agents, and that Yamada was planning to marry her in Japan as quickly as possible, now that she was about to bear his child. Etsu, the woman whom Yamada had not deigned to take in his confidence, and whom Noguchi, following the husband, had always regarded as an obedient shadow, a useful piece of household furniture, could, if she wished, turn out to be a dangerous adversary. It was highly unfavourable that Etsu had reason to complain about Yamada.

Noguchi entered the salon. He peered through the chinks of the lowered Venetian blinds, in order to see what Mrs Matulaka, who had meanwhile returned to the annexe, was doing. She was having her hair combed by her friend.

Noguchi pulled open a drawer in the centre dressing-table and fumbled about in the hollow. The papers he was looking for, which, according to his arrangement with Yamada should have been in the drawer, were not there. Pondering, he bit his thumb-nail. In the mirror, hanging askew, he could see himself full-length. After a moment's thought, he began to search the salon thoroughly. He succeeded in finding all the keys, and knew the tricks whereby some of the mirrors and the marble tops of the dressing-tables could be moved aside. Finally, he walked to the sewing-room and interrogated his daughters. When Mr Yamada left, had he taken his briefcase with him? They knew he had not, since it was lying on a chair in the bedroom. Had they seen any strangers in the house, in the salon? Only Mrs Yamada had been there, wrapping some-thing up.

Noguchi instructed his daughters to go home. Alarmed by the hard, intent look on his face, the angry spark in his eyes, the girls hastily found the slippers they wore outside and their parasols of oiled paper.

The neighbours in the annexe stared at them full of sur-prise. The Noguchi girls never left so early.

'That's odd, Non—what's up?' asked Mrs Matulaka. 'That Jap—something made him very cross just now. What, I wonder?'

'He's not at home, is he?' suggested Non du Cloux, coming out of the bathroom, and with two fingers taking from a saucer the last bits of Lidah Boeaja juice, which she then rubbed into her scalp.

'Neither is she.'

'She's run away!'

Mrs Matulaka protested as though shocked, but de-lightedly, and Non, fired by this familiar game, described the fall of Mr Yamada, inevitable if he no longer had his wife to work for him.

It was already dark in the street, and in the gardens with their ill-kept plants and shrubs. Laundry hung on the line in the backyard: two purplish-grey kimonos of Mrs Yamada's. Their wide sleeves made them resemble hides, stretched out to be tanned.

When Etsu entered the house from the back veranda, Noguchi was waiting there. He gestured with his head to indicate that she should follow him. Yamada was sitting in the salon. His hair hung over his forehead in disarray; he had loosened his collar. He seemed unable to speak. Etsu gave him a quick glance. His bloodshot eyes made his look take on a reddish gleam. Noguchi asked her where she had been. She replied courteously that she had taken something to the Van der Vleckes.

Yamada sprang up, but said nothing. What had she taken there, Noguchi wanted to know. Now Etsu smiled. Her gaze rested on the centre dressing-table, where lay the contents of drawers and compartments hastily emptied—a rich assortment of scissors and clippers, *flacons*, pots of brilliantine, piled up in great disorder. In her thoughts, however, she saw the sluggish brown water of the Molenvliet Canal, in which the clippings and wads of paper and the strips of film negatives cut into pieces had just disappeared, slowly, slowly, but quickly enough to allow her to deliver, exactly at 6 o'clock, according to her promise, a party dress at the Van der Vleckes for one of the children celebrating her birthday. Noguchi looked at Yamada over her head. He ordered her to leave them alone.

'She's back, Non,' said Mrs Matulaka, unrolling the curlers from her hair, now dry. In the growing darkness, Etsu took the clothes from the line. She carried them to the outbuildings and kept herself busy there for a time.

'Poor little thing,' began Non du Cloux, but she swallowed her argument about yielding too readily to male arrogance when the lights in the kitchen and the ironing room went out, and Mrs Yamada, like a grey spectre, glided by on the way to the house.

In the middle of the ceiling of the Yamadas' bedroom hung a naked electric light bulb on a long wire. Wherever Etsu stood, she could always see her shadow on the white walls. From under the bed, she took out a flat cushion and kneeling on it, she now removed the pins and combs, one by one, from her hair. She shook the soft light strands over her shoulders. She then carefully closed the box containing toilet articles, and brushed her hand over the lid. She rested her hands, with the palms down, on her knees. She did not have to wait long. She saw in the mirror how her husband entered the room, followed by Noguchi. Mr Yamada carried a narrow shiny article in his hand—a pair of scissors?—a razor? Silently, he handed it to her.

In the middle of the night, Mrs Matulaka shook her housemate awake.

'Do you hear that, Non?'

In their bare feet, they stole to their back veranda and peered through the hedge. The sky was clouded. In the distance, in the dark, something moved in the Yamadas' backyard. They heard sounds like the thrust of a spade, the thud of falling earth. They held their breaths.

'The Lidah Boeaja,' said Non du Cloux, in a muffled voice.

'But why?' whispered Mrs Matulaka, indignant, plaintive.

'Ah, you know she never liked it!'

'But why so secretive, Non?'

'Oh quiet, be quiet!' hissed Non. She did not know what to answer. Even *her* imagination failed her. Her whole body trembling, she pulled her friend away from the hedge. Breathing a sigh of bewilderment, she kneaded her back softly with one hand.

'We'll plant a new one, here, in our yard,' she said, shrugging her shoulders. 'Those Japs! But never mind—let it be!'

An Affair (Egbert's Story)

LAST week, quite unexpectedly, I saw her in the theatre: Mrs Van H., who twenty years ago had been my father's 'lady friend'. Although she was older, of course, she did not seem to me to have changed. That is, the general impression was the same: thin, a narrow, proud neck, eyes that were large, dark, melancholy, and everything but naïve. She was still wearing those ear-rings that I had then looked at in astonishment, since I could not understand how a woman would, for her pleasure, hook such weights in the thin flesh of her ears. Perhaps that was what disturbed me most when I saw her again: the incessant pendulous movement of something green and shiny along her cheeks, just as in those days.

I was suddenly back at Goenoeng Hidjau, on the sloping lawn in front of the annexe. She lay on the garden chair in shorts, with a folded, three-cornered scarf knotted around her upper body to serve as a bra. I already knew everything. The woman in the lounge chair, with her small breasts, the deep hollow between her collar-bones, her palish brown skin glistening with sunscreen oil (she kept rubbing herself in, with languid, careful movements)—I could not imagine her in an embrace. I found her ugly. When I thought of my father and her together, I did not know whether I should burst out in loud laughter or in tears like a small child. Simon and Doree and I lay not far from her on a mat, in the shade of the garden parasol that was to protect her head and shoulders. The green discs slung back and forth on their thin chains when she moved. On a table to the right of her, she had magazines, a thermos jug containing fruit juice, and a gramophone. She played records of Tino Rossi one after the other, uninterruptedly: '*Dis moi le secret de tes caresses, la raison de ma faiblesse aupres de toi.*' Even then that *chanteur de charme*, with his perfumed sugary voice, made me sick.

The old repugnance came back, in the theatre, when I greeted her from afar; I had an orchestra seat, and she was in a box, and her face stiffened in astonishment, or was it shock, when she recognized me. I resolved to accost her, to ask her what I have been wanting to know for such a long time—do you still think about my father? How was it then, really, between you and him? For even though I realized as a boy that she slept with my father (Simon had told me, and besides, once, sitting at my bedroom window, I had been an inadvertent witness of a nocturnal scene between my parents), I did not know the really important things, the background, the how and why. Tino Rossi sang 'Marinella', there, at Goenoeng Hidjau, while she leaned back with her eyes closed, softly humming along.

Down below, on the edge of the lawn, streamed the *kali* (river). The water glistened among the rocks. The mountains were blue and violet. If you held your head aslant, you could see in the ridges and peaks the profile of a man with his mouth wide open. Jesus, how my father screamed in the last hours of his life: 'I don't want to die. I don't want to die.' It was not the dying itself, but the way he ended his life. He pleaded, he howled for mercy. I do not think he suffered any pain. He must have suddenly realized that his life was over. He clung to me, as though I could help him. And yet, we had not come closer to each other in the camp. I very seldom came to the barracks of the older men; I was with other boys of my own age a little further up, in a row of shacks of woven bamboo, between the Japanese quarters and the fence of the adjoining kampong. Simon did not experience all that; when the war broke out, he had already been in Europe for a long time.

Looking up at his mother, in the theatre, I recalled that I had not seen her since the farewell at Priok in '93, when the entire Van H. family left. Simon's father had cancer, but we children did not know that. Simon was not overly enthusiastic about going to Holland. Glum, with his mouth half open, the corners of his mouth turned down, and an intentionally empty, dull gaze from under his thick eyebrows, he hung over the railing, to make us understand how he felt. Throwing streamers, like the others who were leaving, he regarded as beneath his dignity. When the ship drifted away from the quay, he raised his hand in salutation. He cast a glance at my father. 'Simon looks bad—he'll pick up in a cold climate,' said my mother, fat in a flowered dress, waving energetically. There were spots of perspiration under her arms. Mrs Van H. greeted us with her fingers only; she held her hand and arm straight, her elbow bent; exactly as she waved to me in the theatre.

She was wearing sunglasses, as usual, which made her face, with shadows under the cheek-bones, resemble a death mask. My father must have taken that parting very hard. From then on he was gruffer than otherwise, at his best obliging, but coldly so, and often irritable and absent-minded. I remember the smell of his study, where I then had to come more often than before to be subjected to one of his scoldings: the strong smell of polished wood and insecticide. My mother always bought, at auctions, furniture from the time of the Dutch East India Company, which she then had done up and prepared against termites. The room where my father sat alone, reading and working, when he was at home, was full of such low, wide chairs and benches, with twisted black legs and seats of woven bamboo. There was space enough for a meeting or a reception, yet we had very few visitors. I did not notice that at the time, but now I know that my father was not liked by his colleagues and business associates. Just before Holland was occupied by the Germans, we received news that Mr Van H. had died. My father grew restless then. Now I understand why: he wanted to go to Holland, to *her*. His retirement was still two years away. Perhaps he was walking around with plans for divorce. In any case, he was remarkably silent with regard to the what, where, and how of our future life in Europe. The war, the Japanese Occupation, brought everything to an end. Our family broke up. My mother ended up in a women's camp and my father and I were interned together in B.

During the intermission, I went upstairs to the foyer to look for Mrs Van H. She was standing alone, away from the crush at the buffet, smoking with the same eager intentness as in those days. She held her cigarette between her thumb and forefinger, and let the smoke stream out of her nostrils. She looked absently over the heads of the other people. I went up to her and extended my hand.

'Egbert!' she said, with her wry, ironic smile. I saw her gold eye-tooth shining between her lips. When she turned round to tip the ashes from her cigarette on a saucer behind her, the vague bitter fragrance of her perfume drifted towards me—I recognized it, and it was this, more than anything else in her appearance, that took me back to the things of the past.

Behind the annexe of the Van H.'s on Goenoeng Hidjau, the toilet and the bathroom were in a separate structure: walls of woven bamboo and a tin roof above a cement floor. There were no windows, only a hole for ventilation. The bamboo did not extend all the way to the ground, and between the cement and the ravels of the wattlework, the daylight filtered in in a thin line. Once in a while, during the siesta hour, I shut myself up there, to be able to read, out of reach of Simon and Doree, who always wanted to play, preferably checkers or twenty-one, which I thoroughly disliked. Once Mrs Van H. came rattling at the door: 'What are you doing in there, Egbert? Is there something wrong with you?' I felt embarrassed, being in retreat, mostly because of the ideas she might entertain about it, and I called back to her that I was coming out at once. She walked back to the house from the bathroom, over the narrow veranda that connected this part of the outbuildings with the annexe. The bitter fragrance of sandalwood hung in the air behind her.

While I was speaking to her in the foyer of the theatre, I saw what had previously remained hidden from me: in spite of her withered face, her thin frame, she still had that *je ne sais quoi* that made you think of her first of all as a woman: an ambiguous charm, a mixture of indifference and elegance.

'I never understood how you could like Tino Rossi,' I said, after asking about Simon (an engineer in Brazil) and Doree (divorced, living in Enschede), whom I had not seen since the Indies. She showed no surprise at my turn of thought.

'Oh, no?' she asked, with raised eyebrows and again that ironic smile, taking a cigarette case out of her bag. I gave her a light.

'*Merci*, Egbert. Yes, those *chansons*. They *were* sugary, weren't they? Ah, that was a craze of mine at the time. Remember our annexe at Goenoeng Hidjau? You liked it there, didn't you?'

I asked her, before she might start on the usual reminiscences, 'How long had you actually known my father when I was at your place ... I mean, when did you first meet each other?'

The green ear-rings flashed along her cheeks, and with the tip of her tongue she licked a crumb of tobacco from her lips.

'Oh, a long, long time ago,' she replied slowly, 'when he was still single. He often had his meals at our house.'

My father: a real 'greenhorn', pale and blond in his white suit with stiff collar and wrinkled trouser legs that were too short. That old photograph of him lay in my mother's linen closet; I smell the fragrance of camphor and sachets whenever I try to recall that picture of him as I never knew him. A young face, arrogant, and at the same time innocent. In that form, he had once existed. Astonishment at the reality that can no longer be recovered is suddenly—as so often—mixed with forgotten imagined impressions of my parents' bedroom, the only place where I got to see that photo. The shutters closed against the heat, the blurred shining of glass things on my mother's dressing-table and of the silver hooks that held up the *klamboe* (mosquito net). Strong smell of carbolic acid solution in the small tin containers under the legs of the cupboard. The smell, too, of linens bleached in the sun, rising in waves from the flat whiteness of the bed with its fat round pillows and *goeling* (bolsters). Even then the photo was already faded, mounted on a piece of grey card-board, with the name of the Japanese photographer in the lower right-hand corner. Behind my father stood a palm on a small cane table.

I heard Mrs Van H. repeat that my father often came to their house and that they had gone through 'the whole af-fair', 'that miserable business with Olga.... Didn't you know about that? Ah, no, of course not—you couldn't have known,' she corrected herself quickly. She shrugged, and blew out smoke with her face turned aside. I saw the ten-dons of her neck, and her collar-bones under the black lace.

'Yes, Olga, such a pretty girl. A craze of his. She didn't want to let him go when he had had enough of her. She cut her wrists at our house, to frighten him, to get him back, do you understand, she didn't really mean to take her life. *Enfin*, everything went wrong, a wretched busi-ness. She just lay there screaming, "I don't want to die. I don't want to die."'

My father, on his back on the dirty mat in the men's barracks. I squatted there beside him, my whole body in a cold sweat, not at the prospect of his dying, but at his des-pair, the way he was ending his life. This cannot be, I thought then, Father cannot be like this. He had always preserved his 'attitude', always observed the proper forms. No one knew as well as he the subtle nuances in intonation and forms of social intercourse between superiors and sub-ordinates, equals in rank, people in different fields of work, white people and natives. Once, all in one after-noon, I saw him receive a janitor, a younger colleague, and his chief. From man of authority, he changed into fatherly friend, jovial, but not without a touch of condescension; later the accommodating department head became a pain-fully correct, extremely tense, host. Except on his deathbed I saw him lose all decorum only once in his life; and that was really a comedy.

On the inner veranda of our house, there stood a large gilded clock, decorated with a Knight of the Cross in full armour, leaning on his shield. My father had taken the clock with him from his parental home when he went to the Indies. He was extraordinarily attached to it, and wound it up himself every night before going to bed. From time to time, he would check with one finger to see if the clock had been properly cleaned, or if the shining ornaments on the dull gold of the helmet and coat of mail had not come loose or become bent. One night—I was six or seven years old—I woke up with a start to hear scream-ing and furniture being overturned. I jumped out of bed and walked in the direction of the commotion. My mother was standing on the front veranda with the *baboe*. In the lamplight streaming outside, I saw my father running across the lawn in his bare feet, holding in his right hand the rubber cudgel that he always kept at the ready under his pillow. The houseboy and the gardener kept watch at the gate. The thief—you could hear him gasping for breath hiding among the bushes—no longer had any choice. He dropped the heavy clock and worked himself like a madman over the man's height wall around our yard that was set with glass shards. My father made another attempt to grasp the fugitive's foot, but the man wrenched himself free and escaped. The clock lay on its side in the grass, gleaming dully. The houseboy was about to lift it up, but my father forbade him, his voice cracked with anger. He carried the knight inside himself. His pyjama sleeve was spotted with blood; the thief had cut himself on the glass when he climbed over the wall.

'*Kasihan*, Olga, poor child!' said Mrs Van H. beside me, not looking at me, her thoughts turned inward; what she was seeing was the 'affair' of long ago: new to me, and suddenly unconscionably important.

'My father died in the camp,' I said.

There was no change in her attitude; but I was aware of something rigid and hard in her, like a taut spring.

Once, when I was walking barefoot through the rice fields, balancing on one of the small dikes of mud, now as hard as stone, something flashed and rustled among the young rice stalks. A small greenish snake appeared, flowing smoothly like a living ribbon of water; then, within one second, it stiffened, startled by my presence, into an inflexible ringed spiral. With lightning speed, I grabbed a stone and crushed the head of the snake.

In the furthest corner of my field of vision lay the green spot of one of her ear-rings.

'Yes, I heard that after the liberation. You were with him in B., weren't you? He always wanted so much to go back to Holland. He wasn't happy in the Indies, that father of yours. And now, he's there after all, for good.'

I strained my ears, trying to perceive a sound of sympathy, of regret perhaps, but she maintained her conversational tone, spiced with a touch of irony.

'Once he said, "If I only have the time...."'

She did not finish the sentence, mumbled, '*Enfin*', and bowed in front of me to press out her cigarette, this time in the sand of a flower-box.

We lost the clock with the Crusader during the Japanese Occupation, along with all our other possessions. No, my father had no more time, no time any longer for the golden hours of freedom and happiness, as a gentleman without fear or blame. An impossible ideal, a false blazon, tinsel. As though he, having reached the age that made him eligible for a pension, could have become a different person, able to give up that so carefully donned armour of devotion to duty, maintenance of authority, exemplary observation of forms and precepts. In the camp a different chronology applied—fatigue duty, roll-call, forced labour. Only the Japs had authority. My father was then a man whose ribs you could count, with greyish hair and spindle-shanks in dirty shorts too short for him.

'I can tell you all about it if you like,' I said. She looked at her gold wrist-watch.

'But not now, Egbert. The intermission is nearly over.'

A wave of anger rose up in me, against that self-assured woman so incomprehensible in her aura of sandalwood fragrance; that ugly, attractive, indifferent, coolly amused, elegant, older woman with, in spite of everything, her still sultry eyes: a witch, an aristocrat, the complete antipode of my naïve, serious, stiff-Dutch, ruddy-robust mother. I understood better than ever how enchanting the association with Mrs Van H. must have been for my father, but I knew too that he had been no match for her, that she had time after time slipped away from him, and that he had felt it, but refused to acknowledge defeat. My mother, whom he did not love, who annoyed him, suited him, was the predestined better half of a man like him; Mrs Van H. embodied the other, the dangerous superior, that attracted him but that would always be alien to his inner self. Facing her, I felt the need to stand up for my father whom I have never defended—on the contrary. I did not want to spare her any detail of the horrors of that death, of the end of my father's time to live, of everything that she, with her *Enfin*, so lightly thought she could regard as over and done with.

'One day I'll come to see you,' I said. 'Do you live in town?'

She had taken a small mirror out of her bag, and with the dampened tip of her right ring finger, she stroked her eyebrows.

'For the time being. With relatives, a brother of my mother's and his wife. Perhaps later I will look for something in the South, in Cannes or on the Spanish coast. I don't know yet.'

'What's your address?' I persisted, defying her evasions. ('They're old people, and I'm often away'.) She gave the street and house number—she could not avoid it.

'May I drop in some time?' I asked again, irritated by her unwillingness. My parents were dead and buried. She was still alive. She did not have the right to treat the things of the past *en bagatelle*, as partly mellowing, partly amusing memories of a man with an unsatisfactory marriage whom she had once known intimately and of a boy who had been the playmate of her children.

'Oh, yes, that will be nice,' she said, in a non-committal, conventional ladylike tone. 'I'll show you pictures of Simon and his family. Now I have to go back to my seat. Adieu, Egbert.'

She held out her fingers, but hardly responded to the pressure of mine. I could not understand what possessed her. She made me angry. During the second part of the performance, I looked up at the box now and then, but she was leaning back so that I could not see her.

After the performance, while I was in the lobby reading an announcement of a coming première, an usher came up to me. He held out his hand; in the palm lay a disc of green jade.

'This was found in the cloakroom. During the inter-mission, I saw you talking to the lady.'

'Thanks. I'll return it to her,' I said. The jade felt cool and smooth. The ear-ring was even heavier than I had thought.

*   *   *

It was an upstairs apartment in an old street. On the landing, at the end of the steep staircase, waited the person who had let me in, a servant who had no time or attention for an explanation, and, with no further ceremony, held the door open.

The large dark suite smelled of Indies food: the ever-present aroma of the Indies kitchen, of finely ground chillies and other spices, faint but yet penetrating. Plants filled all the corners, from the window-sills in front to the doors of the balcony in the back; they seemed to be growing wild over the window-panes, filtering the sunlight. There was a screen of carved Japara wood, and the walls were covered with dark blue, brown, and ochre batik draperies, trophies of *krises* and barbed spears, constellations of masks and *wayang* puppets. I had seen many of the objects before, in the Van H.'s house in Batavia.

Exactly opposite the door hung a large painting of the view from Goenoeng Hidjau: the mountain ridge with the profile of a person in an agony of death. Then I saw the very old man and the very old woman, in armchairs on either side of a table with a wrought copper top; they were both slightly bent over and were looking at me as though they had been expecting me. The old woman looked dazed; the man, slight and frail in a robe over his pyjamas, had a yellowish birdlike head, and sharp, distrustful, disil-lusioned eyes. I gave my name and said that I had come to see Mrs Van H. There was a sudden movement in another corner, a door opened and then closed, but not quickly enough. I was absolutely sure that I had seen her, in peignoir and slippers, her shoulder-length hair hanging loose.

'Please sit down,' said the old man. 'Toetie will be with you in a moment. She's getting dressed.'

I sat down. I looked into the burned-out eyes of the really old *neneh*, and at the oriental death's head of her husband. He extended his hand, covered with liver spots, in an almost ceremonial gesture.

'You're —'s son (he mentioned my father's name). Toetie told us that she had seen you here, at the theatre,' he repeated slowly, raising his voice and addressing his wife. She only nodded.

The abandoned, empty nineteenth-century villa named Goenoeng Hidjau, on the slope behind the annexe; half-collapsing verandas and inner rooms, sagging tile floors, the doors and windows partly closed with broken Venetian blinds; in the backyard a brickwork pond gone dry (once *goerami* and goldfish had swum in it), and symmetric rows of whitewashed pots on pedestals, with palms and rank-growing ferns still in some of them. Simon, Doree, and I

loved to go scouting there. In the village, stories were circulated about ghosts appearing in the old house. Mrs Van H.
laughed at what she called, for our ears, 'some nonsense of
the natives', but her laugh was half-hearted, we knew. Her
grandparents on her mother's side had lived there, she said;
she had spent all her vacations there as a small girl and she
had never experienced anything creepy or gruesome. It
was the spirit of a young woman, said the cook and the
gardener of the annexe (out of hearing of Mrs Van H.), a
girl with long black hair and blood on her hands; a child
from the old house, they said assertively.

'You probably think this room is too full, don't you?'
asked the old man, gesturing vaguely in the air. 'All this
junk: the weapons, the masks—it's really too much, isn't
it? Toetie's father was a pure-blooded Dutchman, you know,
and they're crazy about these things, always collecting—
what are you going to do with them?'

My gaze followed his hand. Above the chair where the
old woman was sitting, arranged against a batik hanging
with floral motifs in yellow and indigo, hung portraits,
framed photographs, some of them already so faded as to
be unrecognizable. I continued to stare at an enlargement
framed in a silver wreath; it was as though someone was
really looking in through a small fogged window, a port-
hole window. A pair of eyes, very dark, under black hair
piled high on her head, a defiant, but at the same time
wounded and melancholy look; a sensual mouth, round
cheeks; a lovely Indo girl out of the past. The resemblance
was unmistakable.

'Mrs Van H.,' I asked, half rising out of my chair. I suddenly understood something about her and her life that
had never penetrated my consciousness.

'Toetie! No, that's not Toetie,' said the old man, almost indignant. 'That's Olga. Dee, he's asking who that is!' (Slowly, articulating clearly, to the woman sitting motionless.)

'Olga.' It was the first—and the only—word that came over her lips, a cracked sound.

'Olga?' I repeated involuntarily.

'Poor Olga,' Mrs Van H. had said in the foyer of the theatre. Everything was quiet. I did not know what I should ask or say. Suddenly, the old man again extended his hand.

'And are you going back to the Indies? To the old country?'

'For the time being, I think there's not much chance of that. But who knows—some day I may go to Indonesia.'

'Yes, that's what we must call it now,' he asserted, with a bitter smile full of disdain. 'Yes, yes. Everything has changed.'

'That's Goenoeng Hidjau,' I said, with a nod in the direction of the large painting, in an effort to distract his attention, to nip in the bud a litany over *tempo doeloe*, the old days. 'When I was a boy I often stayed there with Simon and Doree.'

He did not reply, but continued looking at me. I had the impression that he did not know immediately who I meant.

Finally, he said, nodding, 'Yes, it was beautiful. Our family house, up there. We all went there together. Early in the morning the stable-boys brought the horses out and we went riding, in the mountains.' His voice died away.

'I mean the annexe where Mrs Van H. always stayed during vacations,' I explained, but he did not understand me.

'We have pictures of Toetie here too,' he said all of a sudden. He was not so absent-minded that he had not noticed how my gaze had wandered again to Olga's face, life-size behind the round glass. That 'window' had to be dusty; I could not imagine that those dark shining pupils had faded, passed away, that they were not real eyes, but only round spots on paper.

He pointed to a table full of framed pictures. 'There— yes, there! That is Toetie. The queen of the ball!'

I could not do otherwise than stand up and follow the repeated, urgent waving of that bony hand. Indeed, there was Mrs Van H., in a pierrette costume, with a wide net skirt, a beauty spot painted at the corner of her mouth. She could not have been much older than twenty. On the picture she is sitting on a garden table, with one knee pulled up, her hands coquettishly at her side. Beside her is a small girl, looking up at her full of admiration. There is a clear resemblance; only the child is a dark Indo, and the young girl in the *bal-masqué* costume has the dull white skin and the sharper features of a Creole.

'Our daughter Olga was still small then,' said the old man behind me. His tone was not confidential, rather impersonally communicative. I was suddenly struck by his accent.

'Toetie always came to stay at our house when she went to a party in Batavia. Later we moved to Soekaboemi, and then it was the other way around. Olga stayed with Toetie then, so they could go dancing in Concordia or at the Zoological Garden. Young people had a great time in those days, you know.'

I know. I know all the stories about how life used to be in the Indies. Toetie-in-the-photo (I never heard her

called by any other name except Louise, or confidentially,
Loes Van H.) had pompons on the tips of her high-heeled
dancing shoes. The little girl, with her long black hair, is
leaning on the table with one hand, just by Toetie's right
foot; she is holding her fingers up as though she wants to
touch, or has just touched, the tulle rosette. A fan and a
mask are lying on the floor. Four or five years later, the
child was one of the party.

'Olga, such a pretty girl.' Why not 'my cousin, who was
staying with me'?

'She cut her wrists at our house.'

At our house—that was the home of Louise, Loes
(Toetie) Van H. and her husband. At that time they could
not yet have been married very long. My father, a blond
bachelor in *jas toetoep*, fresh from Holland, often had his
meals there. He went dancing with Olga in Concordia
and in the Zoological Garden. Perhaps with Olga and
Mrs Van H. together, two gay pierrettes. With no stretch
of the imagination can I picture Mr Van H. on a dance
floor. He was at least twenty years older than his wife, thin
and bald; but certainly gentleness and mildness personified.
Mrs Van H. always called him Poppie. So at the home of
Toetie and Poppie, Olga cut her wrists because my father
'had had enough of her'. Why? Had he met my mother, a
young schoolteacher, like himself new in the Indies, bravely
fighting against homesickness, full of diligence and goodwill and lack of understanding, not pretty, but from a solid
Dutch family, an anchor that would bind him to his
fatherland? For her, his betrothed, he had the Japanese
photographer immortalize his white, haughty, innocent face.

A door opened, and Mrs Van H. came in, dressed to go
out, coat and hat on, but with the inseparable cigarette

between her thumb and forefinger. She greeted me as though she had really not known that I was there. I gave her the disc of green jade. Her surprise was genuine.

'*Oom, Tante*, look what he found! Amazing! I really felt bad about losing it. I always wear those ear-rings. A wedding gift from Poppie. I certainly am lucky to have met you at the theatre, Egbert.'

'I've seen the picture of Olga,' I said, turning my head.

'Wouldn't you like a cup of coffee? No? Too bad. I have to leave right away—I have an appointment.' She put out the half-smoked cigarette.

"I'll walk along with you, if it's all right.'

As she went downstairs, she had pulled her glove back demonstratively to look at her watch. She walked quickly, but I caught up with her.

'Were her parents with her when she committed suicide?'

'Oh, no!' she said abruptly, her voice muffled in the fur of her collar. 'Oh, my God, imagine! It happened late at night. We had just come back from a drive, and she was very calm then. I was sitting in the front room talking to Poppie. All of a sudden I heard her scream. She was sitting on the bed, on her heels. I saw the blood coming through the *klamboe*. It was too late to staunch it. The doctor came, in his night-clothes, but he could do nothing. We kept all the doors and windows closed, so the neighbours would not hear anything. The servants stayed with us all night. We made them swear that they would say nothing. When my uncle and aunt came from Soekaboemi, she was already in her casket. Blood poisoning, we told them. Of course, there was a lot of talk about it. I think they know, but they never mention it, never.'

'So it was my father's fault.'

'You said suicide. But that was not what she intended. She wanted to shock him, to give him a scare, you know, to get him back. She didn't know him. I told her from the very beginning, "Olga, he is not going to marry an Indo."'

' "I don't want to die. I don't want to die." He screamed that too, when he was on his deathbed. Why did you never write to him, never answer his letters when you still could have? He was very unhappy because of you'.

Now she looked straight at me, from the side. 'Really?'

'Did you want to take revenge?'

The wind whistled around the corner of the street. She shivered and pressed the fur collar against her cheeks with both hands. She peered past me at the traffic. She remained standing on the edge of the pavement.'

'Listen. Olga is dead. Poppie is dead. Your father is dead. It all happened such a long time ago. What do you want, anyway?'

'I just don't understand.'

She shrugged. 'Olga was in love with your father and he with her—and then with me, and I was fond of him, and so was Poppie. But Poppie was crazy about Olga and later the little boys in the kampong. . . . Don't ask me to explain that to you. The matter is ended. It's all over.'

(Mr Van H., attentive, amused, endlessly patient host to his son's friends. Simon's matter-of-fact statement that so astonished me, after he had told me about the affair between my father and his mother. 'Pop knows. He doesn't mind.')

'There comes the tram. Nice to have seen you again. I'll write Simon about it. And you haven't seen the photos! Thanks for bringing back my ear-ring. You're the same golden boy you always were—just like your father: a knight.'

She smiled her crooked, ironic smile and stepped off the pavement to cross the street to the tram stop. But she turned around once more, and said over her shoulder, 'Go and visit Doree sometime. She's so alone.'

Yes, I went to visit Doree, in Enschede. Doree means 'of gold' or 'gilded', golden girl. When I last saw her in the Indies, when we said goodbye at Priok, she was a tall, browned child, with hair that the sun had changed into a nondescript colour. Now that she is so much older, there is a remarkable resemblance to my father. But she has the eyes of Mrs Van H. and those are the eyes of Olga.

My half-sister: a living symbol of the half-ness that I feel myself, divided between here and there, between the desire for order, the cool clearness of the lowlands, and the longing for the sparkling flash of green at Goenoeng Hidjau.

Glossary

baboe	a female domestic servant, a term now considered derogatory and no longer used
bale-bale	a wooden or bamboo couch or a low platform used as a bed
beo	a kind of myna
branie	(as used by the Indo-Europeans): a daredevil, daredeviltry
desa	a village
djait	a seamstress
djongos	a term for a male servant (houseboy, waiter), used by the Dutch, but now considered derogatory and no longer used
dukun	a shaman, a native healer
goeling	a kind of bolster
goerami	a kind of freshwater fish
jas toetoep	a jacket with a high stiff collar and no lapels
kacung	a native boy
kali	a river
kasihan!	Poor thing!/What a pity!
kebaya	an Indonesian woman's blouse, worn with a sarong
ketan	sticky or glutinous rice
klamboe	a mosquito net
klontong	a Chinese vendor
mandoer	a foreman
Oom	Dutch for Uncle

pici	a rimless cap, usually of black velvet
pikolan	a carrying pole
Priangan	the mountainous area of West Java
rijsttafel	literally, 'rice table'; a complete Indonesian meal, consisting of rice with a number of side dishes
roedjak	a fruit salad with pungent dressing
sado	a two-wheeled horse-drawn carriage
sinyo besar	a respectful term of address for a European or Westernized boy, meaning 'young master', now no longer used
sirih	a betel-nut
selendang	a shawl or stole worn over the shoulder or diagonally across the body
soos	club (from the Dutch 'societeit')
Sundanese	the people and language of West Java
Tante	Dutch for Aunt
waringin	a banyan tree
warung	a stall
wayang	a shadow-play

Cambodia

Angkor: An Introduction
GEORGE COEDÈS

Angkor and the Khmers
MALCOLM MacDONALD

Indonesia

An Artist in Java
JAN POORTENAAR

Bali and Angkor
GEOFFREY GORER

Coolie
MADELON H. LULOFS

Diverse Lives: Contemporary Stories from Indonesia
JEANETTE LINGARD

Flowering Lotus: A View of Java in the 1950s
HAROLD FORSTER

Forgotten Kingdoms in Sumatra
F. M. SCHNITGER

The Head-Hunters of Borneo
CARL BOCK

The Hidden Force*
LOÜIS COUPERUS

The Hunt for the Heart: Selected Tales from the Dutch East Indies
VINCENT MAHIEU

In Borneo Jungles
WILLIAM O. KHRON

Island of Bali*
MIGUEL COVARRUBIAS

Java: Facts and Fancies
AUGUSTA DE WIT

Java: The Garden of the East
E. R. SCIDMORE

Java: A Travellers' Anthology
JAMES R. RUSH

Javanese Panorama
H. W. PONDER

The Last Paradise
HICKMAN POWELL

Let It Be
PAULA GOMES

Makassar Sailing
G. E. P. COLLINS

The Malay Archipelago
ALFRED RUSSEL WALLACE

The Outlaw and Other Stories
MOCHTAR LUBIS

The Poison Tree*
E. M. BEEKMAN (Ed.)

Rambles in Java and the Straits in 1852
'BENGAL CIVILIAN' (C. W. KINLOCH)

Rubber
MADELON H. LULOFS

A Tale from Bali*
VICKI BAUM

The Temples of Java
JACQUES DUMARÇAY

Through Central Borneo
CARL LUMHOLTZ

To the Spice Islands and Beyond: Travels in Eastern Indonesia
GEORGE MILLER

Travelling to Bali
ADRIAN VICKERS

Twin Flower: A Story of Bali
G. E. P. COLLINS

Unbeaten Tracks in Islands of the Far East
ANNA FORBES

Witnesses to Sumatra
ANTHONY REID

Yogyakarta: Cultural Heart of Indonesia
MICHAEL SMITHIES

Malaysia

Among Primitive Peoples in Borneo
IVOR H. N. EVANS

An Analysis of Malay Magic
K. M. ENDICOTT

At the Court of Pelesu and Other Malayan Stories
HUGH CLIFFORD

The Best of Borneo Travel
VICTOR T. KING

Borneo Jungle
TOM HARRISSON

The Chersonese with the Gliding Off
EMILY INNES

The Experiences of a Hunter and Naturalist in the Malay Peninsula and Borneo
WILLIAM T. HORNADAY

The Field-Book of a Jungle-Wallah
CHARLES HOSE

Fifty Years of Romance and Research in Borneo
CHARLES HOSE

The Gardens of the Sun
F. W. BURBIDGE

Glimpses into Life in Malayan Malayan Lands
JOHN TURNBULL THOMSON

The Golden Chersonese
ISABELLA BIRD

Illustrated Guìde to the Federated Malay States (1923)
C. W. HARISSON

The Malay Magician
RICHARD WINSTEDT

Malay Poisons and Charm Cures
JOHN D. GIMLETTE

My Life in Sarawak
MARGARET BROOKE, THE RANEE OF SARAWAK

Natural Man
CHARLES HOSE

Nine Dayak Nights
W. R. GEDDES

A Nocturne and Other Malayan Stories and Sketches
FRANK SWETTENHAM

Orang-Utan
BARBARA HARRISSON

The Pirate Wind
OWEN RUTTER

Queen of the Head-Hunters
SYLVIA, LADY BROOKE,
THE RANEE OF SARAWAK

Six Years in the Malay Jungle
CARVETH WELLS

The Soul of Malaya
HENRI FAUCONNIER

They Came to Malaya
J. M. GULLICK

Wanderings in the Great Forests of Borneo
ODOARDO BECCARI

The White Rajahs of Sarawak
ROBERT PAYNE

Philippines

Little Brown Brother
LEON WOLFF

Singapore

The Manners and Customs of the Chinese
J. D. VAUGHAN

Raffles of the Eastern Isles
C. E. WURTZBURG

Singapore 1941–1942
MASANOBU TSUJI

Travellers' Singapore
JOHN BASTIN

South-East Asia

Adventures and Encounters
J. M. GULLICK

Adventurous Women in South-East Asia
J. M. GULLICK (Ed.)

Explorers of South-East Asia
VICTOR T. KING (Ed.)

Soul of the Tiger*
JEFFREY A. McNEELY and PAUL SPENCER WACHTEL

Thailand

Behind the Painting and Other Stories
SIBURAPHA

Descriptions of Old Siam
MICHAEL SMITHIES

The English Governess at the Siamese Court
ANNA LEONOWENS

The Politician and Other Stories
KHAMSING SRINAWK

The Prostitute
K. SURANGKHANANG

Temples and Elephants
CARL BOCK

To Siam and Malaya in the Duke of Sutherland's Yacht Sans Peur
FLORENCE CADDY

Travels in Siam, Cambodia and Laos 1858–1860
HENRI MOUHOT

Vietnam

The General Retires and Other Stories
NGUYEN HUY THIEP

The Light of the Capital: Three Modern Vietnamese Classics
GREG & MONIQUE LOCKHART

Titles marked with an asterisk have restricted rights.